PRAISE

"Disturbing, poignant and alive with the beauty of human struggle trapped in economic runoff, *One Morning* is a page-turner that ends up haunting the reader."
—Rick Kleffel @ *Narrative Species*

"This elegantly told and thought-provoking work deserves a wide audience."
—*Publishers' Weekly*

"The novel's meticulous construction and its flawless narrative make this a most impressive debut. Warning: Don't read this book alone in an isolated cabin in the woods."
—*Aurealis*

"Twelve chilling stories told over twelve hours in real time, *One Morning* digs under the skin of a Pennsylvania coal mining town to show you the shadows dancing hellishly underneath. Beautiful, brutal, with a strong savage heart."
—Paul Jessup, author of *Daughter of the Wormwood Star*

Also by Jessica Hagy

AETUI: Pentagram Poems
Indexed
How to be Fearless
How to be Interesting
The Humanist's Devotion
The Art of War Visualized

ONE MORNING

JESSICA HAGY

Underland Press

Underland Press
www.underlandpress.com

ONE MORNING

Before

Midnight: Helena

One in the morning: Ruth

Two in the morning: Agnes

Three in the morning: Valerie

Four in the morning: Paige

Five in the morning: Marley

Six in the morning: Eileen

Seven in the morning: Tasha

Eight in the morning: Olivia

Nine in the morning: Amanda

Ten in the morning: Alice

Eleven in the morning: Caroline

Before

Millions of years ago, the Appalachians are as high as the Alps. Water changes that. It dissolves exposed stones, rinses soil down hills, gouges valleys with river currents. The things that live on the mountains die and sink into peat bogs. As a hundred thousand human lifetimes pass, water condenses and falls, flows and freezes, thaws and evaporates, is consumed and expelled. It flattens peaks and fills valleys with the fallen silt.

In the foggy spring of 1829, a man named James Gour surveys a seven-hundred-acre plot of sacred land deep in Penn's Woods and declares it a farm. The soil beneath his feet, soil that once kissed clouds, is tilled even further under. Fathoms below his sharp till, ancient life has turned to flammable stone and waits to be exhumed.

The Pennsylvania Railroad pries open a station in 1842 on land the Gour family had wrestled into orchards. The locomotives stabled at the station gobble coal and belch black clouds. The water cycle spins faster now, accelerated by the heat and vapor expelled by the trains.

A mining company buys the rest of the Gour farm as 1854 begins. A town springs up, the charming Gour Borough: mushroom circles of little wooden houses around the train station and the mine entrances. Men proudly wear streaks of black in the creases of their faces, under their nails, deep in their lungs. Those men dig deep caverns far below the water table to harvest the coal crop, planted millions of years ago. Massive pumps continuously exert themselves to keep the water from flooding the mines. When the coal seams are depleted, the pumps and men retire. As soon as the pumps are silent, the water invades. Below Gour Borough, acidic lakes slosh where the coal had been. That water breaks down all the bedrock it can lick. It leeches heavy metals from the mines and carries them out, back up to the undark surface. The water has found a new way to weaken the mountains.

By 1917, all the mines are officially abandoned. The companies that clawed out the coal have legally evaporated and no person can be coerced into claiming ownership or responsibility. So water lays claims to everything, as it always has. The town remains above the flooded caverns and its dwindling population drinks water weighted with mine-runoff and the long history of collapsing mountains, dissolving stones, and lapping tongues.

The Morning of

December 1st, 2016

Gour Borough

Pennsylvania

Midnight:

Helena

She's stitching yak fur to a yeti mask. Intense work on an impossible deadline: the kind of commissions that pay the most, the most satisfying work she does. She was offered a reality show once, but her introversion convinced her to turn it down. Besides, she thought, who really wants to watch a show about theatrical taxidermy? Ever since she saw her father skin a deer that dangled and dripped from a beam in the garage, she's been under the spell of skins as artistic media: how they define and contain all manner of characters.

It's the biggest project she's had in a while; it'll pay the bills (hers and her sister's) for at least a year. *Tech millionaires and their fetishes*, she assumes. But this one, this one's odd. The anonymous client specifically requested this have three antlers, just like the local yeti-type legend: The Old Man of the Woods. Helena wonders if the client might be local. And it has to be delivered first thing the next morning, at the drop-shipping place out by the parkway.

She sits under a mantel covered in dusty trophies. *Crypto-Taxidermy Grand Champion* (for the unicorn made from a white baby goat's hide and a narwhal's horn). *First place, Mythical Beasts* (for the griffin she composited from the shells of a lynx and a falcon). A *Technical Academy Award* for costume engineering (for a dozen elegantly eerie silicon and mother-of-pearl mermaid tails), a *Lifetime Achievement* (for all the rest). She makes the imaginary seem real, alive, possible.

The magnifying glass helps her thread each strand of fur onto the skin. No glue, all hand-tied knots. She cuts no corners. At the edge of the rooms the costume hangs on a human mannequin. A true hair suit of tailored camel leather. The zippers are so deeply hidden they look and feel like old scars.

Her sister, Agnes, is calling. Again. Helena ties a tight knot and reluctantly answers. She has to. Eight years ago, her niece, her sister's daughter, disappeared. Since then, her sister has drifted further and further from reality and functionality. Helena never says anything when her sister calls. She just breathes into the phone and listens.

She idly strokes strands of yak hair as her sister imparts another theory. This time it's about some massive eagle that swooped down and stole her daughter away to a nest at the top of the world, where the girl still lives, nestled happily between feathers and cat collars and clouds where she lives as a lookout, a goddess on a mountaintop. *But I know that's not true*, her sister sighs.

And because her sister never asks anything of her, never says, *And how are you?* or, *Are you seeing anyone?* Helena never has to tell her about the married man who arranges dates once a month, entertains her but keeps his distance, asks so little of her, who she keeps around purely out of habit. The guy with the outer shell of roughness and brashness and cruelty, who nonetheless grins and blushes when her shadow slinks over him.

She's been seeing him for ten years. She thinks that ten years sounds like less of a milestone than a decade. She's never loved him, but she knows her feelings are reciprocated. He's her hobby. She's his. That's plenty. Actually, it's more than she requires or even likes. She has too much work to do, too much love to put into the skins and pelts and glass-eyed faces to really care for his damp, fleshy one.

He admires her work. He keeps a raven of hers under glass in his study. *A raven for my writing desk.* He's specified in his will that she gets to stuff him once he dies. She told him she'd mount him with a diaper with a bow and arrow and pigeon wings: an elderly, corpulent cupid, and gift him to a museum. He very much liked the idea. She thinks of him, not quite fondly, while her sister rambles.

She says goodnight when her sister has said all she called to say. Helena worries, sometimes, that her sister won't be able to maintain her coping mechanisms forever, that any day now, she'll slide down the wrong side of the sanity curve. There haven't been any leads in the case for years. She worries that if Amanda is ever found (and she knows, that after this long, it's probably a body they're looking for), her sister will lose her sustaining daydreams.

The yak hair is wiry and hard to work with: brittle and stiff. But it looks perfect. The yeti costume is almost complete, just a few more details: file the fingernails of carved cow horn, burnish the waxed-goat leather calluses under the toes. She'll add the antlers last, the crowning details.

She hasn't set a big fire in a long time. She's been trying to behave herself. She's never been caught. She's almost fifty, and never once has she even been a suspect. But she feels the urge constantly. It's an itch in her throat, a sweaty tingle between her fingers. She thinks about how lovely a plume of smoke would look under the low, drizzling clouds.

She works faster. She's earned a flame or two, she thinks, admiring her own handiwork. The antlers are anchored into place with thick sinew, and then sewn around the edges with gray silk. A ten-point buck donated them to this strange cause. She hopes the client respects her work enough not to ruin it completely, at least not right away.

The mask looked somber before the antlers were attached. And now, with them, it's menacing. *A superbly affective creation*, she smirks. She fits the mask onto the mannequin. She aches to photograph this one, even though she signed an NDA promising not to ever share the existence of this commission.

She puts away her tools and materials. She's twitchy to incinerate, to collect her accelerants and her matches, to listen to timber crackle and burn. The first fire she set, she was only seven. She burned down her grandmother's tool shed. It was glorious. When the insurance check didn't bounce, she stopped feeling guilty.

Should she? Of course not. No. Does she want to? Absolutely. But where? Nowhere people are, it has to be out in the woods and weeds, somewhere near her sister's house. Every other house in that valley is boarded up. The population of Gour Borough has halved in the last decade and there are dozens of abandoned places to torch. Maybe someone's long lost cousin can collect insurance.

She knows just the place. She's been day-dreaming about it for months.

Down near foamy Turtle Creek, on the road recently zoned unsafe due to mudslide risk. Where the electricity is off, and the unused sidewalks sprout weeds from every crack. She'd been hiking near there, foraging for moss for her projects, when she saw the place. There's a crooked barn, a black barn, just waiting for her: three stories of luscious kindling.

It's maybe five miles from her workshop. Maybe. All back roads. Very little traffic. The deer-path is at the top of the hill. She can park there, sneak down to the property, splash some gas around. This is not a spur of the moment burn. No, this will take planning. She wants to do it right, to do it carefully. The opposite of a wild fire: a controlled demolition.

She's giddy now, just thinking about it. She'll go tonight, pitch a neon-blue tent near the property like she belongs there. A reconnaissance mission. She'll go, look around, let the excitement build. She hasn't looked forward to something so much in quite a while.

She's never told anyone about her fires. Never. Not once. Should she tell him? They're meeting for lunch. She could. He wouldn't say a word. If he did, she could call his wife. She decides against it. She'll take no risks with her precious, splendid flames.

Daydreaming must run in my family, she mutters as she remembers the deadline. She still has a lot to do before the yeti's ready to ship. She has a coffin-sized crate waiting to hold it in her garage. She has her camera in her cabinet. And she has a full gas can. And some rags. And her trusty silver lighter. She happily snorts and sews more yak hairs into place.

It's almost finished. The more details she embeds in a figure, the more alive it seems. She knows her work is done if she feels pity when she looks into its eyes. The reflections in the brown, murky glass make the eyes of the mask look like the yeti is recalling painful moments from childhood. Perfect. She pats the mask on the forehead, soothing its emanating anxiety.

She went down to the stream that runs red with iron runoff and smells sulfury like a bad omelet, and brought back just enough dark, coppery stain to make the tips of the fur look roughly lived in. She rubs it in, staining both the fur and her fingertips. She knows, based on the pages of details in the client's instructions, that this is a suit needs to look as real, as wild, as possible. She handles her work with the respect of a mortician.

The suit was made for someone only five foot two. The yeti looks juvenile at this height, even with the extra foot of antlers. Usually she gets instructions on these kinds of jobs about the sex the costume needs to project, but not with this commission. Maybe it's not a fetish object? Maybe it's for a bored housewife who wants to scare the hell out of her neighbors.

She lays a hand on the shoulder of the yeti. She feels more empathy and appreciation for the creatures she assembles than for the people she knows. She gulps back a tear for the melancholy yeti. This is why she could never do a television show. She has trouble being around skins with souls inside them, unable to feel they're as real as the characters she creates herself.

Anyway, buddy. Time to go to your new home, she says as she wheels the costume down her hallway. Her home isn't decorated as much as it is simply full of her work. The living room is her sewing workshop and photography studio. The kitchen is used for mixing dyes and tanning leathers. The oven holds a box of assorted lizard skins. The pantry's full of leathers in every shade of clay. She doesn't cook.

The spare bedroom's a hoard of feathers, buckets of glass eyes, and piles of fur scraps: a walk-in-at-your-own-risk closet. In her bedroom, a stuffed badger sits by the window, reading *Playboy* through a monocle. He wears a tartan vest and a gold watch chain. There's a Canada goose reading over his shoulder: beak open, tongue lecherously out. Her stuffed animals stand in for friends.

The pine crate's lined with pillows of cedar chips: protective and aromatic. Any box takes on the aura of a coffin as soon as a human-sized costume goes inside, and she doesn't mind the imagery. She places the costume in carefully, folds the gnarled hands over the chest, and places more cedar pillows over the top. Her commissions are destined for other homes: to her, wounded creatures that are lovingly rehabilitated and then released back into ungentle wilderness.

She raises the hammer to nail the wooden box shut, and then sets it down gently. She can't wake the neighbors. It's the middle of the night and the architect who put this house together was stingy with insulation. Like so many houses in Gour Borough, hers is too close to an abandoned mine land (AML) to ever sell or bother fixing up. Her liability of a house is cold year round, and tilts to the east thanks to its sinking foundation. She'll finish in the morning, once she hears a few alarm clocks chirp.

Maybe just a candle? Maybe just a little flame? Yes. Just a bit. Just a little. Then try to steal some sleep. She fumbles for a jar of wax, sets it on her bedside, and lights it. She feels relieved. She wants more. She can go, she thinks. No one will know. She shakes her head. No, not tonight. It's too late.

But the candle is so beautiful. Stop. It's been sleeting out there for days. It would take forever to start anything. All the wood is wet and slick. The badger looks over his monocle judgmentally. He's why she never brings that man into her bedroom. She'd have to throw a towel over the badger and the goose.

Despite silently scolding herself not to, she decides to go before dawn. She thinks of her favorite fires. Backyard sheds. Abandoned strip malls. The dock that fell right into the lake. The abandoned duplex down the street from her sister's house. Her secret hobby has caused over seven million in recoupable damages.

She has a car just like ten thousand other cars. A little sedan: gray, rusty and unassuming. Bought used after its first owner defaulted on the payments. An angular, rusty Toyota Celica, so long out of warranty it's hard to find parts for the thing. No feisty bumper stickers. It runs, but not quickly. She'll drive below the speed limit and use her signals. She's never been pulled over.

She has tidily bobbed, graying hair and unpainted fingernails. She wears roomy, unloud clothing, sensible shoes: the aura of an accountant rather than the artist she is. She is unnoticeable in the way that women become when menopause begins and catcalling quiets. She blends into the background of any place she visits. She knows she was right to decline the television show.

She shuts off all the lights. Blows out the candle and watches the red wick blacken. Leaves the crooked screen door dangling open behind her as she hops to her car. Opens the Toyota with the quiet of the key, not the beep of the fob. In the trunk: clean rags, the gas can. In her purse: a silver lighter, full of fluid. She is always prepared.

She tries to start the engine. Nothing. She growls and huffs. The universe is telling her not to burn down that barn. She hasn't changed the oil in three years, a fact she doesn't even consider as an issue while she curses the vehicle. Her skills lie in the creation, not maintenance, of inhabitable objects.

In the passenger seat is a bag of findings, pieces and parts she picked up at the Goodwill. She's not afraid of many people, but the Goodwill proprietor gives her shivers. *Helly, I've got some great toad skins for you. Toad skins and some arm-lookin' bones. Child-sized ulnas. You'll love 'em.* Helena doesn't know how that woman sources her odds and ends. Doesn't want to: the back-stories of real people hold less potential for her than the backstories of lush, tanned leathers. She grabs the bag and shuffles back up to her porch.

Helena lives on the side of a steep hill with nicer views of what's left of downtown Gour Borough than her property taxes suggest. Down the street is an unsanitary butcher shop. Up it is a dim tavern where unwise decisions get made with regularity and resolve. She had her parking spot-sized lawn paved over five years ago, so she didn't have to mow it anymore, and it's already cracked in half and home to dormant goldenrod as tall as she is. She reaches into the bag and the edge of a toad skin, dry and sharp as an X-Acto blade, slices her hand open.

She growls and huffs again. Bleeding, she stomps inside, wraps her hand in rags. She knows how to take care of herself: silently and without a fuss. Instead of whimpering she wrinkles her nose. The stoic, quiet, self-sufficient child who can look after herself and her siblings—she's been that kid for almost fifty years. Blood is soaking through the rags and dripping onto her knee. It's a sharp, deep gash. She sees the bright side: She's worked with less-pliable leather. It's just another dermal seam to knit into invisibility.

She runs her right hand under hot, tea-colored water from the tap, purses her lips but does not shout. A two-inch gash in the meat of her palm, a new line for a palm reader to interpret. *Your pain line, it's deep and jagged, doesn't quite connect your index finger to your thumb. It says you have terrible taste in automobiles and men.*

She selects a roll of slick black silk and a dusty bottle of whisky from an overflowing cabinet over her sink. She finds just the right antique silver needle, a sharp little dagger. She sterilizes the needle in the whisky. Gulps the polluted shot. Threads the silk. Pours and gulps another mouthful. She begins to close the seam.

An expensive cosmetic surgeon would have made twelve stitches, close enough together for the cut to heal flat. She knits her flesh together with twenty even lines. She knows she would have done an even more meticulous job if she'd been able to sew with her dominant hand. She feels strangely warm.

She dabs a bit of ointment—expired four years ago: but you build with the blocks you have—on her work and finishes it with a fabric scrap. She hears the tavern regulars shouting and stumbling down the street. Somebody knocks over a garbage can and glass shatters on pavement. Somebody else musically combines a belch and a cackle. They've seen better days, but they still love their nights. She smiles with her lips together. The badger and his monocle are not amused.

She ponders the bag of frog skins and yellow bones. She doesn't think about the silence in her house, about the lack of contacts in her phone, about her missing niece, about the way her knees creak when she walks upstairs, about the fire she didn't get to start in the sleet.

She needs work to do, or she'll really have to burn something down.

Having no work left to occupy her, she navigates her piles of art supplies through her house, sits outside on her front steps. She pokes through the plastic bag of dead things she paid seven dollars for. She's not sure if she got a deal or a swindling. The frog skins are tough and brittle, potentially useful but not in a way she can identify yet. The narrow bones, bones she sincerely hopes are not human, are barely the weight of pens in her hand. Those fragile things don't call out a purpose to her either.

She spins a bone in her fingers like a tiny baton. She points it at the dribbling sky. She stretches her feet. Her head feels heavy now. Her eyes are tired. If she was a prayerful person, she might have prayed for something then. But she never learned how to ask for what she wanted from anybody on any plane of existence. Her wounded hand is throbbing.

A mask. A mask to filter smoke. That's what she'll make. A mask like a medieval plague doctor: a long, beaklike filter to keep particulate out of her lungs. It will be frightening and elegant. Oh, yes, and big, flat glass lenses for the eyes. She smiles. Thinking about work is much less difficult than thinking about the rest of her life.

She listens to the sounds of the neighborhood. The joking smokers outside the tavern, the sound of cars driving past on the main road at the top of the hill, the furnaces humming up and down the street, the white noise of the endless sleet. She imagines it wouldn't take much to ignite the entire, crumbling avenue, once the clouds slither away. Every neighbor would get an insurance check: eventually, hopefully.

She didn't take anything for the swelling: doesn't have any gulpable medicine (other than whiskey) in the house. Her skin presses taut against the bandage. She peels it away, and lets her stitches breathe in the damp night air. She turns the skins over and over in her hands, feeling for where she would carve a seam, where she would affix and strap, which skin should fit alongside her eyes and which edges would align best with her forehead.

The toads, when alive, secreted a buttery poison from their skins to deter predators. Mystics from long-decimated societies once licked such skins to get closer to God. Traces of it transfer from their skins to hers, into her blood through her cut. She begins to see images forming in the illuminated rain around the streetlights: animals, landscapes, vegetables, faces: the shapes a functional imagination can pluck from clouds and folded ink blots. Her breath is cool and foreign in her mouth. She wiggles her toes. They feel webbed inside her ugly, sensible shoes.

She sees the universe for what it is: a slag-pile of jagged, unintended consequences, grinding each other into the past. She feels her own atoms spin in their orbits, and she giggles—she has not giggled in almost nine years, not since Amanda disappeared. She hears her own breath and it sounds like the punch line to the greatest joke ever told. She is laughing so hard she slips down three porch steps, scraping along the wet concrete.

The patio she lands on begins to wobble. The world is going soft all around her. No angles can stay right. The air is now chowder-thick. She imagines herself as a flame: an honest thing that laps up fuel without greed or regret. There's a wading pool full of dirt and broken Christmas lights left up for three years on the property across the street. She sees those details as perfect in their context, that they're as much part of the town as she is. Why change when you're perfectly acceptable where you are?

And yet, there's so much she never was. She's suddenly sad that she never grew any feathers. She wonders why there are no black owls, purple alligators, or spiders big as dogs. She mourns those things that never existed and promises to make them from the skins of things that did. When she dies she wants everything she owns to be burned and the ashes compressed with absurd technology into a diamond her sister can pawn.

She takes her lighter from her pocket and flicks it awake. The little flame winks at her, and she winks back at her intermittent pet. Her hand is throbbing, but now the heartbeat of her swollen thumb and the heartbeat she hears between her ears are out of tune.

She rests her head on the rusty iron railing of her front stairs. She understands that it is there to help her, that it was installed there thirty years before precisely for the purpose of supporting her skull at this very moment. She knows she is where she belongs, where the universe has placed her. She hopes her niece is somewhere well-insulated and cozy.

She makes a loose fist with her throbbing hand, straining her stitches. Orange plasma oozes out and she thinks of mosquitoes trapped in amber and dinosaurs drowned in tar. The clouds are moving fast above her head, commuting to work in faraway fields and forests. She coughs from laughing at the idea that clouds are as honest and free as fire.

She closes her eyes and lets a warm sensation spread out from her spine and she wonders if this is what it's like to be wise. She does not feel her immune system raging against the mischievous poison or her blood cells popping inside her veins. She does not feel herself aging and dying, cell by cell. Her nerves do not register the heavy metals lodged in her bones and teeth, souvenirs from a childhood spent frolicking in foamy, opaque streams.

She hopes the little antlered yeti isn't frightened, lying there in her garage. She silently promises it that, soon, it will be just where it belongs, just like she is. Some soul will climb inside it, and its skins will contain life again. She hopes a theatrical woman will wear it to terrorize a Peeping Tom away from every window he walks past.

Her body defeats the toxin without her knowledge or permission, dissolving it with the chemistry of immunity. The unreal colors behind her eyes fade and the world she sees begins to solidify and lose its hallucinogenic sparkle. As her heartbeat settles, she climbs back inside her crooked house, shakes the metallic dew from her hair, and decides to rebandage her dominant hand.

One in the Morning:

 uth

Ruth thinks that the farm where they've been imprisoned is some-where in Pennsylvania. She is correct. They're in Gour Borough, population five hundred eighty (give or take), a plot of land that commerce sampled decades ago then spat out. Ruth is from a place she can't remember the name of anymore. She's thirteen. Her fellow captive, Amanda, is sixteen. They could easily be mistaken for eight- or nine-year-olds. Ruth, barely a teenager, weighs only seventy-seven pounds. Neither one has seen a newspaper or a tele-vision show or the inside of a book since they were taken. Ruth has forgotten how to read.

Ruth very much regrets opening that car door. When the preacher pulled up beside her and told her that she had sheep and bunnies to pet and a cotton candy machine in the kitchen, that she'd just made fresh applesauce and couldn't eat it all herself, five-year-old Ruth had no idea what she was climbing into. The preacher has kept her in the limbo of a livestock barn so deep in the woods that nobody who could help has ever heard her crying. The preacher is a negligent shepherd. Some days, Ruth is fed and given blankets. Other days she is ignored, chained in a stall like the other sheep in the barn.

She does not believe the preacher's words, not since that first lie, but she believes in everything else. Everything else. Ruth believes in infinite universes: that all things are possible and really happen-ing somewhere and somehow. The idea managed to find its way into her head without any words attached, while she lay still on a concrete floor.

Before she hopped into the preacher's car, her mother told her bedtime stories. She believes the story of the two circus bears. A trapper captured two bear cubs and while one fought and snarled, the other sat silently and plotted her escape. The quiet, cunning bear secretly clawed metal shavings from her single chain while the other cub earned more confining chains for her protests. The loud, feisty bear cub was fitted with five metal cuffs: one for each paw and one around her neck while the quiet, still cub was only trapped by one. Then the quiet cub broke her single chain and escaped, while her honest sister did not. The moral of the story: don't make your own life more difficult.

And so, she scratches at her chain with the edge of a flimsy fingernail. She's been scratching at it for almost eight years, rusting it slowly with her sweat. At first, she scratched furiously. Now, absentmindedly. She wears an iron cuff around her ankle that clanks when she runs away in her dreams. She shares a barn with several sheep and only that one other child. Amanda is feistier, angrier, and stronger. That girl wears three chains, like the loud bear from another universe.

Somewhere else, bears talk. Somewhere else, Ruth is at school. Somewhere else, she rides horses and wears silver bracelets. Somewhere else, her mother is a queen who drives a golden Cadillac. Somewhere else, it is impossible to tell a lie to a small child. Somewhere else, she has not broken her chain—but in this universe, she finally has. After all this time, she's succeeded at breaking it apart. In another universe, she would cry happy tears.

In this one, she exhales quietly and begins her escape. She has not eaten in several days, and when she stands up, she wobbles, dizzy. She steadies herself and creeps across the dirty floor to the barn door and takes a ring of keys from its hook. She squeezes them so that they do not clatter. A sheep shifts in its sleep and grunts. She moves to the stall where the other girl, the noisy bear, is curled up and sleeping, and unlocks the chains that tether her to the wall.

The other girl is startled, then shocked, then relieved, then unable to stop grinning and crying into her fists. *Quiet, Amanda. Be quiet. Please.* Ruth speaks so rarely that the words require awkward effort to create. Ruth does not know what to do next, not exactly. She has a plan that extends only to the edge of the farm, but that should be far enough. *We go to the train yard. Someone who can help us.* Ruth leans against a wall to steady herself. She feels like she might faint, but she knows that now, of all times, she cannot. She unlocks the shackles that tether the sheep to their walls, too. They do not thank her for their freedom.

She leans against the barn door and lanolin-smeared hinges swing silently open. Four sheep and two girls hobble out into night and sleet without alerting the one authority they all fear. The preacher told them that she is a prophet, someone who God confides in. Ruth thinks the preacher is crazy, because nothing she ever says makes sense in any way. Ruth thinks it might be something in the water: it's bitter and tea-colored and slippery to drink. She wonders if she's crazy too, if everyone is, and she's relieved to think that in some other world, every-body's a genius.

The preacher tended and sheared her meager flock haphazardly. Years ago, she seemed more attuned to the needs of her pets. Years ago, there were dozens of sheep. Only four have survived. Lately, the preacher can rarely be bothered to peek inside the filthy stable. She's been growing more and more unpredictable, more sedentary, more confused. Ruth knows that in some other world, the preacher is an Olympic athlete, medaling in every event.

In almost any another universe, the preacher would have taken her role as shepherd more seriously. In this one, the girls and sheep sleep in the same dirty barn and chew on the same rotten animal feed. The malnourished girls sometimes roll clods of dirt around in their mouths, desperate for fuel. The preacher sleeps in the other building, the house designed for humans, where she eats stale cereal with filthy hands.

In another universe, Ruth and Amanda would not find the winter night so painfully cold. In this one, they are dressed in dingy pillowcases with ragged holes for heads and arms. They have no shoes, but they do have thick calluses. They wear itchy, filthy woolen blankets. They have no more than a quarter inch of hair on their heads. *God*, the preacher told them, *is punk rock*, and roughly sheared them with the same clippers she uses on the sheep. Ruth is missing a half an inch of cartilage off the top of her right ear.

Ruth remembers crying when she was hurt and being soothed instead of scolded. She remembers having pigtails and eating popsicles and being kissed goodnight on her forehead. She does not remember her mother's entire face. As she flees, as always, she hopes that she will recognize her when they are reunited, and that her mother will know her.

She points toward the train yard, just south of inert and foamy Turtle Creek, the creek where the sludgy water flows. That's the direction they should go. They know the trains are there, but they've never seen them, only heard the rumbling of the heavy cars. Frost coats the field grasses in tender glass, glass they can melt with their feet. Ruth can handle a few cuts, a few bruises. More than a few, if need be. She will gladly pay all the painful prices to be kissed on the forehead again. She leaves red-streaked footsteps.

Even when I'm not watching you, God probably is. God watches the news too. God can watch her own mouth, because she has eyes everywhere. God knows a lot of stuff, the preacher cooed, as she would chain them up. Ruth assumes nobody is really watching her in this uni-verse: they would have done something if they did. No one notices her running through the woods. No one sees her holding her arms out into the darkness, reaching for something, fending off branches. No one sees the quiet bear hobbling through the sleet without a chain.

She will never wear wool again, she promises herself. She will never chew on dehydrated corn kernels or sleep on dirty straw. She will let her hair grow long. She will sleep with both legs free to kick. She has no destination in mind, but she is happy to go where trash and criminals and trains all go: Away.

The edge of the grazing yard is ringed with rust-frosted chain-link fencing. It's not high, but it is crowned with barbed wire. Tufts of wool trapped in its links prove it to be a formidable barrier for the sheep. But Ruth is not a sheep. She pulls the blanket from her shoulders and throws it over the fence. She climbs over it, toes pinched between the links of the fence and motions for Amanda to do the same.

A wooded ravine separates the preacher's property from the railroad tracks. When the town had a population of a few thousand, it was the local dump, but decades of fallen leaves have hidden the secrets of the town and its trash. Ruth hasn't been this far from the concrete barn in eight years. Low brambles pull at her pillowcase, at her blanket, at the skin of her arms and legs.

She's aware that the sun rises in the east and sets in the west. She does not know if she is west or east of her mother's home or if it is still where she left it. She knows that if she can hop on a train, she will go somewhere better. Everywhere is better. Away is ideal. She is patient. She is the quiet bear. She grits her teeth and slips down the muddy hill. Her hands and feet are numb with cold.

Her right ankle feels flimsy without the shackle around it. Her balance is off. She feels like she's stumbling, but she is making forward progress. Amanda is stronger, larger than she is. Ahead of her, Amanda offers her a hand and helps Ruth up the last few feet of the ravine. The girls had been kept apart, forbidden to touch or speak. Ruth feels the warmth in Amanda's hand and shivers.

At the top of the ravine, the girls look back toward the farm. A light is on. The preacher. She's awake. She might hunt them again. The girls listen for sounds of motion, eyes wide and mouths still. The preacher does not move quietly. She will stomp like falling thunder towards them, if she moves at all. Hearing nothing but dripping sleet, they continue.

A more formidable fence, eight-feet high, rings the train yard. Signs posted every dozen yards: NO TRESPASSING. Ruth thinks of another bear story, a dark joke the preacher told. Two campers are running from a hungry bear and one turns to the other and shouts: *We have to outrun the bear.* The other camper laughs: *No, I just have to outrun you.* Ruth knows Amanda is stronger than she is. Ruth does not let go of Amanda's hand.

There: a few yards ahead. A low space between the bottom of the fence and the earth. A wormhole to another universe. There are lights on the other side, shining on the tracks. Ruth feels like she is out of time, out of place, a character missing from all the pages it's supposed to fill. The rocks are jagged on the girls' bellies. The bottom of the fence claws at their backs. They've crossed into another realm.

An office? A sentry? A lookout? There has to be some-one here. Someone on duty. Guarding. Protecting. But no. Guards cost money: money that shareholders would rather have. The train yard is a quiet parking lot anyone can loiter in. A mile to the north of the girls, one conductor is sleeping in his bunk above his engine. He will move his train soon, but not soon enough for Ruth.

The girls feel exposed under the bright lights that shine on empty boxcars. Behind them, they hear their tormentor thundering up the wet hill. The preacher is shouting, *God hates sneaks! God hates thieves! God hates quitters! But God really loves a good game of Ping-Pong!* The girls crawl underneath a boxcar, hoping that it does not begin to move.

The girls have bloody feet. They've left bloody foot-steps. They shouldn't be hard to find. But the preacher is slow. She's half blind and without a flashlight, and there-fore unable to notice such details as red footprints in frosted grass at night. Ruth doubts the preacher can climb over the little fence. She knows she's too big to slip under the taller one where the girls did. Ruth hisses to Amanda, *She won't find us.* Amanda whispers back, *But she found us before.*

The preacher's shouting is growing fainter. She is roving and raving in the wrong direction. Ruth knows that in another universe, they would be yanked from under the boxcar by their ankles and dragged back to their moldy barn to sleep on straw frozen into bricks by sheep urine. In another universe, the preacher is nimble and agile and can hunt them by smell. But Ruth is not in any of the other universes. She is under a boxcar, breathing shallow, quiet breaths.

Amanda climbs out and hisses, We have to find some-one. She begins walking on the side of the train, toward the engines, toward someone, anyone, who can help them. Ruth watches her but does not follow. She will not be taken back into captivity. Ruth is the cunning, not the noisy captive. She will let the hungry bear catch the first camper it scratches.

There are at least a hundred train cars, all snaking north. Ruth wants only to slip inside one and ride to Away. Amanda wants to find a tender, beating heart and convince it to take her directly home. Ruth wonders if her tendency toward extreme caution is a virtue or a vice, if she is truly cunning or merely timid. Her world is dark, and her eyes strain to find light in it.

Ruth can't hear Amanda's footsteps any more. She doesn't hear the preacher either. She hears her own heart-beat though, and it's unsteady. If she hadn't scratched at the weak link in her chain, she knows her heart would flutter and stop eventually, like a bird that's crashed into a windowpane. But it can't stop yet. Not yet. She climbs out from under the boxcar, determined to never return to the barn.

No train stays in one place forever. No train full of cargo waits for long. *This train will move soon enough*, Ruth thinks. She does not know that her mother lives only three miles away. She does not know that when the preacher had snatched her, she'd been driven in a huge loop on the interstate. She does not know that on that drive, the preacher had considered taking her home, had felt bad about the abduction, had briefly reconsidered, had not yet entirely trusted the voice of God in her head. In another universe, Ruth would have been in the preacher's possession for just a few hours. She would have been home for dinner.

Ruth pulls her blanket tighter around herself. She'd been five. Her mother had been tucking her in. *So, do you know how much I love you? As much as the whole universe! It never stops. It just goes on and on and it has everything in it. That's how much I love you.* And Ruth had gone to sleep happy. The next day, she got into the preacher's car, excited to pet a sheep and see a cotton candy machine spin sugar into floss.

There's space enough for every idea, maybe not in the world, but somewhere. *Somewhere*, she thinks, *there's a boxcar I can climb into and sleep.* That somewhere turned out to be the one she had been hiding under. Ruth wonders if that God was finally watching her, if that God had taken pity on her and gave her just what she wanted. If God really had put an empty car there, just for her. *No*, she thought, *Not God. Just someone who works at a train company.*

The corrugated metal floor is rusty and cold. Her bloody feet stick to the frozen metal, and so she wraps them in her foul scrap of blanket. She watches her breath turn to vapor. *The train will move. I will go away from here. Someone will find me. Accuse me of trespassing. I'll say my name, say I'm missing. Say I want to go home. And I will. I will. I will.*

There were glow-in-the-dark stickers shaped like stars on the ceiling above her bed. There was a purple radio that played happy music on her nightstand. There were different clothes for waking and sleeping. There were purple shoes instead of gray calluses. A toilet with blue water instead of a pile of briny straw. And she was going back there. To that world. To her parents, who had made sure all those things were there, who had faces Ruth could almost see if she shut her eyes so tightly she cried.

She was about to dream, to visit a different, cozier universe behind her eyelids, when she heard the shouting. That gritty, angry voice. She covered her mouth with her hands, to hide the clouds of her breath. *God hates sneaks! God loves roller skates! God knows you're not ready for Primetime!* The preacher punctuated every sentence by banging her fist against the side of a boxcar. Each approaching echo of unmusical percussion made Ruth's heart wobble faster.

Think. Think. Think. If she's out there banging around, then she doesn't have Amanda. Amanda is nearby. If she finds me, she will take me back to the farm. Just me. She can't drag us both. She isn't strong enough. But if I can hear her, so can Amanda.

You live with someone in close quarters for long enough, and even if you are forbidden from speaking, kept away from each other with chains, you get to know them. And so, when Ruth heard the preacher scream, then heard a dull thump, and then listened to the long silence after, she knew without seeing what had happened. Amanda, the honest bear, had gotten her honest revenge.

She hears Amanda crow from a few boxcars away, *Got her! Got her!* Ruth is not relieved. She is not upset. She is not surprised. It all makes sense, in this world. She peeks out of her hiding place and sees Amanda panting and beaming, standing over the preacher's crumpled body, a rock the size of a loaf of bread wedged between the preacher's meaty shoulders, Amanda with her own shoulders back and her hands on her hipbones.

Ruth took eight years to scrape through one link of chain. Amanda took eight seconds to bludgeon the preacher. They had saved each other, as best they could. Ruth smiles in the darkness of the universe she's doing her best to navigate.

Ruth hears a diesel engine grumble awake in the distance. She hears the chains that link the boxcars rattle and strain. She feels a pull beneath her. *Come on, get in. Get in!* she manages to say. Amanda dashes toward her and jumps aboard. Neither one looks at the preacher's body, a colorless, lumpy thing in the mud, as the car creaks past it. *God's going to need to find a new buddy now,* snarls Amanda with a dirty grin. Ruth exhales in the dark and closes her eyes. She is almost unconscious, not almost asleep.

How will sheep survive the winter untended? Will the preacher's body be found by coyotes or people first? Ruth isn't sure if the God of this universe thinks about such things, if he thinks of them at all. She wonders if in some other world, the preacher's God feels lonely because his prophet, his chosen friend, is suddenly missing.

Amanda sits near the door and watches moving darkness. Ruth is curled on the cold metal floor, unable to see anything but the rock on the neck of her kidnapper. *Is it wrong to take one life so that two others might get theirs back?* Ruth shuts her eyes and asks God, any God, in any universe, for answers. Nobody replies.

The boxcar rattles, a chamber of noise. The girls do not know how broken they look. How thin, how gray, how frail. They did not know what other people look like anymore, or that other people would be dressed in so many more layers, so many more colors. They do not realize that the first people to see them will gasp in horror and pity and confusion.

Ruth doesn't know that her father still staples posters printed with her face onto phone poles. She doesn't know that her mother still dusts her room and changes the sheets on her bed every week, just in case Ruth's on her way home. Ruth doesn't know that the person who recognizes her first is still entitled to a ten-thousand-dollar reward.

She feels the train slowing. How fast can a train go? How far has she traveled? Does she need to hide in the rumbling box for hours or days? As it slows, it passes behind the house her mother lives in, where her mother sits, unable to sleep, watching television, trying not to think about Ruth while garish commercials flash.

The girls learned how to sleep in shackles, and how to be silent, and how not to talk back, and how to ache and want without complaining. They did not know what they had failed to learn, being locked away on the preacher's farm. Ruth, despite herself, feels guilty for breaking that link in her chain. She hopes the rock didn't hurt too much, when Amanda crashed it into the preacher's dense neck.

What happened to the bear after he escaped her confinement? Where did she go? Was she welcomed back by the other bears in the woods? Or was she tainted? Made untouchable by captivity? Did she feel badly that her brother remained in the clutches of the circus master? In what sort of universe could that cunning bear ever be happy? Ever sleep without a nightmare? What kind of world would that be? Wind dries the blood on Ruth's feet. She has trouble holding up her head, and so she lets it fall.

The train comes to another stop, connecting more cars at another small depot. They're nestled between low mountains, out of moonlight's reach. Ruth has no sense of time or distance, and her eyes can't focus in the dark. Amanda waves to her, says something about finding help, kisses her on the forehead with raw lips, and hops out of the boxcar. Ruth silently wishes her all the luck in all the worlds.

For too many years, Ruth and Amanda orbited each other but never touched. Ruth knows that in another universe, their paths are elegantly braided together, and they look each other in the eye and see more than their shared fears reflected and feel closer than twins.

Ruth tells herself that she is patient, not weak. This is not her stop. Her stop will be where people are looking for her, where people are waiting. The cunning bear knows that no boxcar can stay empty forever. Someone will come to her. No need to risk any journeys into the slippery darkness. She pulls on her sheep urine-soaked blanket, but it does not block the cold.

She tries to imagine the texture her hair will be when it grows in, what color it might be if she were someone else, in another universe. She imagines herself wearing a long fur coat and a crown of rubies. She pictures Amanda, healed and nourished, with black hair longer than trees are tall, and a smile of pearls.

I don't know where my home is. I don't know. But other people will. My mother will know. When the railway workers find her, they will call the police. *A child. Eight years old. Maybe Nine.* Her mouth will not form words. Her hands will not reach out to accept help. Her picture will be everywhere, but her mother will not recognize it, not at first. The train lurches forward.

In this universe, her father will know her face instantly. He will see his eyes and nose and funny ears glowing at him from the television. He will nod and point and clap and scream. He will call his ex-wife. He will tell her to turn on the television. *Yes, now.* She will pause the image and stare at it. Press her nose to the screen. Make eye contact with the artist's sketch. Eventually, she will admit that is her daughter's face. And Ruth's mother will weep into the phone. Ruth curls into a tight, angular ball.

In some other universe, it is summer, not winter. In another universe, the train car is full of plush pillows, not noise and wind. In another universe, her cuts are healed. Her bruises: faded and painless. Her ribs: hidden under a layer of firm, healthy flesh. Her memories of the preacher, lying there on the tracks with a stone on her skull: erased. Ruth does not move.

She knows it's winter. She knows the ground is covered in frost and mud from days of sleet. But she feels so hot. Her blanket feels heavy. She throws it off. Her skin tingles with strange warmth. She does not realize it, but the cold has settled into her bones, tricked her brain into sensing imaginary heat. Her small body cannot keep itself warm any longer. She closes her eyes and imagines that she is a huge bear with dense fur and ample energy to last her an entire winter.

In her last dream, she sees the best of all universes. Her old room. The nightlight at the foot of her bed that paints the walls in honey-golden shadows. Her blankets are scented with lavender fabric softener. She snuggles into a stuffed bear with a velvet nose and bright glass eyes. Her mother strokes her hair and hums to her. *That's how much I love you.* Ruth moves her feet, and no chain clatters. She exhales. She is home: in the correct universe again.

Her body pulls the blood away from her extremities. Her brain goes slack and her mind's eye closes. Her hands and feet fade to blue. Her heartbeat slows. Even when asleep, she is strategic, cunning, resourceful. But not cunning enough. She is too small and too thin. As the train rolls on, her eyes freeze shut.

In another universe, she awakes. It's a bright, warm morning. There are pancakes on her plate, maple syrup in a little pitcher, just for her. Cartoons are on the little television in the corner of the kitchen. The Christmas tree is upright in the living room, but it's not decorated yet.

In that dreamy world, she will climb onto her dad's shoulders to perch the angel on the top of the tree. Her mom will help her string the lights so the wires don't show. But in this universe, the one without any talking bears or bare but fragrant Christmas tree, a flashlight shines into her boxcar. The flashlight is dropped. Authorities are called. Before she is zipped into the bag, an artist sketches her features and she is given a last name, for now: Doe.

Two in the Morning:

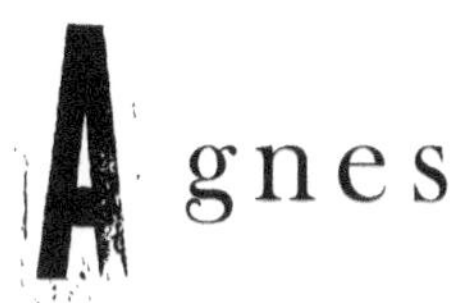

gnes

She goes for the lamp. It's the kind of blatantly gaudy thing only an unjaded little girl could love. A golden pole impales the trunk of a rearing, plastic unicorn, its mouth frozen in a silent scream. When plugged-in, the unicorn glows from its belly, like it has a bioluminescent intestinal parasite. It's garnished with a frilly purple shade. Amanda adored it once. It will be satisfying to destroy.

Two thousand nine hundred twenty days since her daughter disappeared. And on every one of those days, Agnes destroys something. She needs to break things, every day, or she'll explode. Anger and sadness congeal into one destructive emotion because she keeps them hidden from everyone, including herself.

It started with smashing a plate: a piece of smooth white porcelain shattered across her red linoleum floor. She found such calm in the breaking. So she repeats the process. Whenever she felt the need to obliterate something (which is whenever she thinks of Amanda), she wordlessly does.

To Agnes, an object has no value beyond how deliciously satisfying it will be to obliterate. It is the only utility she acknowledges. If a thing will splinter, shatter, unravel, rip, or crack: it holds potential value. But beauty, rarity, sentimentality: they no longer register as resources worth conserving. Her destruction is not creative; she simply smashes.

She doesn't replace what she'd destroys. She just brings home trash bags to collect and banish the aftermath. By now, her house is full only of echoes. She doesn't let anyone visit. Not that anyone knocks on the door anymore. Her house is known to be haunted.

She still hopes that somehow, in some far-fetched twist, Amanda might be alive and well somewhere. But after eight years, if that was true, then Amanda doesn't miss her, doesn't need her, doesn't care to come home, doesn't know or remember who she really is anymore. Even the best-case scenario is awful.

If she had just run away, if she had found a happier life without her mother, if she was really some happy sixteen-year-old living some glorious life: then why not open that door? Why not step into her room? Why not break everything in it, just like everything else in the house? Why not smash that stupid lamp she loved?

If Amanda's not coming back, she won't need the unicorn lamp. Won't sleep under the pink paisley bed-spread. Won't wear any of the little girl clothes. Or shoes. Or coats. Won't play with the toys: those faded old plastic things that will shatter into so many brittle shards.

Only a nonbeliever desecrates a shrine. It's taken two thousand nine hundred twenty days, but that's what Agnes has finally become: a nonbeliever. She does not believe Amanda is coming back. And there are so many objects in that room she can shatter.

She hasn't been inside that room in years. She thought before she went inside, *When I open that door I will be overcome. I will be overcome with memories. I will scream and cry and it will be too much.* But she underestimated her long-practiced numbness. She was unmoved by a room full of items that were her daughter's treasures. When she looked into her daughter's dusty and temptingly shatterable mirror, a blank face looked back. The room smells stale.

Amanda's room is stocked with things Agnes has mostly forgotten about. Things no one would miss if they disappeared. A room full of dust and clutter and trash that spiders have knit together. She's momentarily disoriented when she steps inside, as if she's in the entirely wrong universe. She snatches the lamp from its dusty table and flees quickly. Everything behind the door she slams shut is doomed.

She'll take the lamp to the back alley and whip it by its cord into the gravel over and over until she feels better or it's in pieces too small to break down any further. She never really feels better after a good smashing, only exhausted in a slightly different way.

She keeps looking at it, trying to feel some sadness or loss, some nostalgia. But instead, she's irked by the tackiness of the thing. By how yellow the once-white plastic is. By how, no matter how cherished a thing was once, eventually it will become creepy trash that nobody wants. She knows how estate sales and lives end: with full garbage cans.

She turns on the porch light, and sees a deer standing in her bedraggled backyard. It's one of those freak deer. With three antlers. Like something her sister would make into a puppet. They say it's because of the heavy-metal rich wastewater leaking from the long-ago abandoned coalmines. They say that the mineshafts have flooded and are now spilling vile molecules all over the water table. They say that now tree roots suck up the chemicals and feed old poisons to every leaf-eating thing in the forest.

They are the EPA, and they're just guessing. There's no money to ever really know for sure.

That's the reason she drinks water from bottles and can't sell her house for any price to anybody. It's built on top of a coal mine no miner has been inside in a hundred years. The basement's always damp with viscous orange water. The foundation is porous from marinating in acidic groundwater. She knows it's the reason Amanda only had three fingers on each hand. She knows it's why businesses close and families flee. That it's why the people who are stuck here swallow so many pills. Drink on so many Tuesdays. Inject into so many veins. Smash so many hollow unicorns.

But why didn't Amanda come home? A kidnapper snatched her. A trip and fall and amnesia. An eagle carried her off. A circus caught her eye. She learned to fly and reached the moon. She rode off on a unicorn that hadn't yet turned yellow. Joined a cult, a sorority, a multi-level marketing scheme, a silent marching band. She was only eight. She was only two thousand five hundred twelve days-old.

The deer flicks its ears and lowers its head to graze on dormant crabgrass. It's that time of year, when the rifle shots ring out. When the freezers fill up with venison. Agnes never owned a gun. Never shot an arrow or a bullet. But she wants to swing that lamp and knock out the deer. It's a greater sin to break something beautiful than to damage what's already ugly. And her guilt feels sharper than sorrow, and thus easier to embrace.

She is an old woman ready to swing a plastic lamp like a medieval flail. She is shoeless and listless in the middle of an alley in the sleet on a winter night. She is wearing clothes she's already begun to pick apart. Her bones are old and lacking calcium but rich with cadmium. Her skin is spotted, dry, and not a freckle of it has been kissed in a decade. She looks lifetimes older than her forty-five years. The deer chews calmly. He's not yet noticed her standing there.

She only speaks to other people when she goes to the grocery store every other week, and when she calls her sister to ramble and be heard but not listened to. She says very little to strangers. *Cash. No coupons. Paper bags. You too.* When she calls her sister, she cups the phone with both hands and whispers into it. Her voice is raspy. Her hair is matted. Her eyes are unfocused. Her muscle tone is slack. It's amazing how slowly a body pivots toward atrophy when its mind lacks a reason to go on.

She watches the deer. Before her shadow falls across his flank, he's alerted to her presence. He raises his head. The whites of his eyes are briefly visible. He makes a pained, guttural sound and bolts away, into the dull hiss of sleet, as if shot with a police Taser. Agnes barely blinks at his recoil.

Get a pet. Join a support group. Put yourself out there. Find a therapist. She'd taken none of that unwanted advice. Nobody knew what she was feeling and thinking. If they did, they would be terrified. She had instead turned in on herself, growing smaller and more brittle. Silently, secretly aching for Amanda, who, for some terrible, unknowable reason, is surely, permanently gone.

The alley is silent except for the droning sleet. No creatures rustle between weeds. No birds sing night songs. Agnes freezes. The forest is afraid. Of her? No. Of something even worse. She drops the lamp, splitting the unicorn in half down its ragged, plastic seam, shattering the light bulb in its stomach. The rumbling begins.

Worms and roots rise from the soil. Pebbles hop along the top of the alley. Stubborn leaves get shaken loose from branches. Puddles ripple. She sucks in cold air and stands steady. Another section of an abandoned coal mine collapses and warps the shape of the hill behind her flimsy, wooden house, pulling trees at odd angles, cracking her foundation with fresh, jagged lines. She's never been so close to a mine collapse. She wishes she could break so much so quickly.

She leaves the cleaved lamp in the alley. The earth has defeated her. Everything is so much greater, so much more complex than she is. Hidden caverns flood and empty and slosh and cave in without her permission. People all around her advance in age and knowledge, sometimes both, without her consent or awareness. Trees and weeds and spiders multiply without her blessings. Everything goes on, heedless of everything else that doesn't.

Hers, like at least a million other homes in Pennsylvania, is situated on what her former insurance company refers to as Abandoned Mine Lands (AMLs). The deep, hollow caverns fill with groundwater that turns to a ravenous, acidic soup: a metallic puree that devours the bedrock: geological osteoporosis. And so the sinkholes pull down the foundations of so many towns. At least the mines under Gour Borough are flooded and not on fire. There's an underground fire burning out by the airport. Nothing will grow on top of it and animals won't even walk across it. If it keeps burning, the air traffic control tower might topple over and burn, and then nobody could fly away. Agnes grinds the unicorn's half-head into the gravel with her bare, cracked heel.

Agnes breaks things. She keeps that to herself. Her sister burns things. That's a secret Agnes isn't supposed to know. But she's smelled the gasoline on her sister's coats, seen the ashes where there shouldn't be any. She knows that whenever there's a local blaze, her sister doesn't answer the phone.

Call her back? Ramble on about Amanda? Then, give her a gift. Two gifts. One: the secret that she is destructive, too. And two: an entire house to burn. *Oh yes, hello. I'd like to tell you that my home is bare because over the years I've been smashing everything I own into the tiniest possible pieces. It's an empty house. And you know I can't sell it. So, yes, well, uh, would you like to bring some gas and some rags and—?*

And then what? Go and live in her sister's overflowing museum of creepy-faced taxidermy? She'd be too tempted to rip apart the stitching, strip furs down to bare hides, pluck glass eyes from wool sockets, unravel satins and yank lace apart. She'd be the worst kind of houseguest. She whips half a unicorn down into gravel.

She must keep herself to herself. She is someone people avoid looking at. She is too sickened by tragedy to pretend that the world can be a decent place, and she is rightly assumed to be contagious. People avoid her because they worry her despair is contagious, and they're correct. She drops the cord.

She goes inside, sits cross-legged on the floor in the middle of her living room. It was wallpapered, once. An off-white, subtle print of ferns and butterflies, rows and rows of them, swirling all around the room. Fifteen years ago, it had been quite stylish. Four years ago, she ripped it off inch-by-inch, until her fingernails bled and a layer of sanatorium green lead paint was exposed.

She hears something, no, someone, on her front porch. A flashlight shines through the filthy front window, scanning. Did she lock the door? No. She never does. The knob turns. Unlike the deer, she does not bolt away.

It's a teenager, thin, dirty, greasy ponytail under a bright orange cap. His jeans are too big and they're dark gray from knee to floor. His sweatshirt hangs from him like a shroud, wet from shoulder to waist. She knows the type: seduced by some dream that won't love him back, lost, with the eyes of a rabbit with its leg in a snare. A ghost with a heartbeat and crooked teeth. Kids like these are Gour Borough's best-known export.

Welcome, she says. And she sees that he's terrified to find her there, to be greeted by someone inside an abandoned-looking house. She realizes she looks like the antagonist of a horror film. The mad crone sitting alone in the empty room. The thin witch waiting to shove plump children into her pre-heated oven.

I didn't think anybody lived here.

If you want to call it that.

What?

Living. If you want to call it living. You're only looking for a place to be, not live. Right?

Yeah.

This place is fine for that. The guest room's upstairs.

And she crookedly rises from the floor to lead the damp boy to her girl's dry room.

The boy tumbles onto the bed and mumbles a thank you. With a shower and a solid meal, and maybe twelve years of unrelenting, unconditional love, he might be able to lead a decent life. She leaves him to sleep, or whatever it was he's doing with his eyes shut on the dusty, paisley bedspread. *Good night*, she says as she closes the door. She means it, but she doesn't feel it.

Squatting sounds so fecal, so dirty. But squatting is precisely what happens when people abandon their homes to the whims of the crumbling mine shafts beneath their foundations. The police cover the windows with plywood. Paint big red Xs on the doors. Let the mice and birds and spiders take up primary residence. Give up and give the acidic, crumbling bedrock time to make the right angles acute and the architecture wobbly. The vagabonds invade next. Demolition costs money the county doesn't have.

So many years, and she'd left that room untouched. Until tonight. That boy needed that bed. Needed that disintegrating pillow. Needed a mother to tuck him in. A dreary echo of what happened in that room some three thousand days ago, when there was still a light inside it. Before she stole the light to shatter in the back alley.

That boy must have a mother somewhere. A mother who worries about him, even if he makes her furious. A mother who wonders where he is, how he is, if his wounds are healing. Agnes should ask him for her name, her address. Agnes should let her know her son is alive and unwell. She feels useful, just thinking about that. Finally: a job to do other than cash her disability checks and take her mutilated trash to the low curb.

She goes to the basement, where she keeps her photo albums in a plastic box near the furnace. She reaches up to yank the metal chain and a naked bulb casts shadows on the cobwebs and moldy, slaggy walls. She hasn't looked inside that box in at least a thousand days. Groundwater gone bad pools beneath her feet, acidic drainage from the abandoned mines that will continue to corrode for generations. Trauma always echoes longer than the unharmed think it should.

She opens the box, sees pictures of herself, pictures of herself with Amanda, and she cannot believe she ever looked so young. And her sister. Her sister looks impossibly young, too. But then, her sister always looked child-like: like an elf, a fairy. With that mischievous smirk that's turned into a sneer over tedious time. Her sister: a hothouse flower planted in Penn's cold woods.

There: the pictures of just Amanda. Plump. Happy. Full of enthusiasm for glitter and unicorns, her smooth braids secured with clean ribbons. Amanda with her blood full of the chemicals that give the tap water its unenviable terroir. Over time, Agnes has learned to see the shape of her daughter's teeth with photographic clarity, all the little angles and details of the enamel. Mental dental records, just in case.

Agnes does not need these things anymore. Pictures of so many dead, lost people: including herself. These pictures aren't memories anymore. They're just heavy papers she doesn't want thrown into a trashcan after her estate sale concludes.

Important people leave legacies. Small people leave evidence. Agnes doesn't want to leave any. Doesn't want anyone to look at a pile of trash on the curb and pity her. Her estate is not a hollow mine that she can just abandon and hope other people find the time and money and initiative to clean up. If she can destroy everything, there will be no mess and no estate to settle: there's nobody to leave anything good or bad to, anyway.

Amanda had three fingers on each hand. That's another way Agnes would be able to identify remains if they were ever found: those Gour hands. Amanda's best friend was born with the same deformity, and nobody knew exactly why, but everyone guessed it was the water. In Gour, you could blame anything on the water, and everybody would agree with you. Agnes never saw Amanda's hands as deformed. She thought Amanda had the most beautiful hands. She could look at Amanda and see what exactly a little girl was supposed to look like.

Agnes gathers up the photo albums and trudges up the sagging basement stairs. It's time to get rid of these. It's time to stop trying to remember details that won't ever be important. Time to destroy the evidence that she once held so much unrealized potential: both in her smile and in her arms.

There's a lighter in the corner of the back room Agnes pilfered from her sister's home a year before. That room is where Agnes wrestles with insomnia most nights, on a bare mattress, having years ago picked her bed to splinters. She snatches up the little flame-maker. She understands her sister's affection for fire. She can't bring herself to rip apart Amanda's hundreds of paper faces, but the flames will dissolve them for her. She clenches the lighter like a stolen jewel and dashes outside to use it.

In the weedy alley she drops the photo albums onto the gravel. She adds the broken lamp and its tacky shade. Her gnarled hand holds the lighter to the unicorn's fractured tail. It takes a dozen flicks of the lighter to catch a flame in the soft rain. She sighs with complicated relief as the photo album sizzles.

Across the alley, another deer. This one is unantlered, female. Deer season is far too short to keep their numbers at ecosystem-sustaining levels. This doe is small and timid, but Agnes can see her watching the flames. That landslide rattled the ground with shallow earthquakes, and yet, just a few minutes later, the animals resumed their nocturnal grazing. It all goes on, and so quickly. A flimsy bit of ash floats upward. Amanda's baby pictures will become ash, become soil, become leaves, become the flesh of deer, become the flesh of venison-eating people. Nothing remains itself for long.

The boy in the girl's bedroom is disoriented and uneasy. He doesn't know if he dreamed the old woman, how he got to the place he rests. He realizes he's afraid. He just wanted to find a dry building, so he didn't have to set up his tent in the rain. He wasn't expecting such spooky hospitality. He sits up, looks out the window, sees a fire and a deer and he feels like he's a character in some folktale he was assigned in high school but never read.

Agnes wiggles her bare toes into the sharp gravel and watches the unicorn melt, watches the plastic sheath around the power cord bubble away and the wires inside glow red. She watches the deer move through long, smoky shadows. Amanda's smile glows orange, then melts to black, then disappears. She has another stack of things to burn tonight.

The next stack of papers all say the same thing: MISSING REWARD $10,000. How many of those posters did she hang? How many faded pages did she remove and replace over the years? At least a thousand. She bought boxes of staples for the staple gun. She impaled every staple into corkboards and electric poles. At first, she had a lot of help. She stopped hanging them when she was sure enough time had passed that Amanda couldn't possibly look like the face printed on the posters anymore.

The face printed on them is the one she will always see when she imagines Amanda. The school-picture smile. The cocked head. The long hair in two, even braids. The smile with only one front tooth, the other hiding in the gums, unready. She can't picture her daughter any other way. If the skull was ever found, she'd know it instantly.

In the basement there are thousands more of those posters. Faded yellow, like the unicorn. Agnes will burn them all tonight. Her sister would approve this destruction of the evidence that she'd given up so much hope. As she rids herself of more possessions, she feels a little lighter and further away from herself. She feels clean and hollow, like a fallen sparrow's dry skeleton.

The boy rises. His clothes are still wet with sleet. He's always ending up somewhere. Always finding himself in places that don't match where he wants to be. He doesn't draw a clear line between real and ideal experiences anymore. Everything is simply as it is. He runs away, so often, but never finds his desired, proper Away. He wanders on foot. He knows that if he had a car, he wouldn't feel so lost, could reach his fate faster.

He should be going. He should be heading somewhere else, trying to find a place that will make him feel more useful or maybe even strong. He feels like a trespasser in this house, even though he was invited inside. He'll go where things are better: Away. Or at least, he'll try to.

But first, he'll thank the crone for her hospitality. There was nothing predatory, nothing menacing, nothing unsafe about her.

He was only looking to stay out of the sleet. Only looking to be away from home long enough for his mother and her boyfriend to resolve their latest fight. He hoists his backpack, heavy with a dry change of clothes and a pilfered six-pack of beer, over his shoulders. Walking away always feels better than staying where he feels he doesn't belong. He is always on the move.

The deer picks her way back into the woods, nibbling at leaves infused with slag and sulfur. Agnes does not recall when she last ate. A day? Two? She pulls a blade of crabgrass and wads it in her mouth. It's bitter. That's fine. She feels very much of the place: fed and watered, carved and eroded by the environment.

Agnes gathers another armful of posters to incinerate. The yellowed paper is still sharp along the edges. Agnes feels the sting of a dozen paper-cuts in her forearms. These stinging drops of blood are proof she's not entirely hollow, not yet. Her ability to register sensations hasn't atrophied entirely. She's reassured she still exists by the subtle pain.

Can I help you? asks the boy, as he stands at the top of the basement steps, watching Agnes lug heavy paper around in the dim. He'd wanted to slip away unnoticed, but he's instinctively helpful.

You can.

Okay.

Together, they carry up a thousand yellowed copies of Amanda's gap-toothed smile to burn in the alley. He knows who the gap-toothed girl is. She's the ghost that haunts Gour Borough. She's the reason he wasn't allowed to play outside alone when he was in elementary school. That's Amanda. He remembers. She was in his kindergarten class. He doubts his mother would offer to pay a thousand dollars for him, if one day he just didn't come home. He feels warm pity for the crone. She traces the word 'reward' with her finger and sighs, *I still have that money put away. Just in case. Probably fine to spend it now.* He looks away, sadder than she is about what she just said.

Well, thank you, he says for the hospitality that unnerved him, as he turns to walk into the darkness. Agnes, unused to conversation, blurts, *Tell me your mother's name and address.* She has authority in her posture, if not in her voice, and he replies to that, clearly and submissively, as Agnes crumples another poster into the fire. By the time he has trudged out of reach of her firelight, she's forgotten the answer he gave her.

Three in the Morning:

Valerie

How long has she been lying in the shallow nest of sharp gravel, in the vicious sleet, in the dark? There is a brittle pain at the base of her skull. She struggles to sit up. She grunts, wipes drool and dirt from her face; fights to remember how she got here. Yes. That. That's what happened. The children were here. Or was it something else? Her mind is not what it once was, or what it's supposed to be.

She's in a train yard. Next to a track so cold, if she licked it she'd merge with it. A place down a steep hill from the sheep's grazing yard. A short walk, if she can manage the incline. She thinks she can get there. Home. She hears God rambling again. *Old age is a small price to pay for not dying.* The voice feels both loud and far away, as if it's shouting at her from across a frozen lake.

She began hearing God's voice when she was twenty, some ten years before. It was quieter then. The voice did not come from the throat of a deity, but from a tumor, smaller than a grain of rice, tucked behind her right eye, above her right ear, inside her skull: benign only in the medical sense. As the tumor grew, God's voice grew louder, stranger, drunker. God's megaphone is now the size of a tennis ball.

The children were spoiled. Yes. Spoiled. Not with too much, not with gifts and attention and compliments. No. Spoiled like milk: left alone and untended. Gone sick and slippery. Congealed into unappealing globs. She could have fed them more often, but she was always forgetting. Could have given them more of something like affection, but she had no idea how. And now they've up and gone to who knows where. *Did you know that ninety percent of*

American women wear the wrong size bra? God asks her. She does not answer. She never answers.

She's wet with sleet. Soaked through her wool coat and thick socks. She has not changed her clothes in weeks. They smell of the sheep she tends, their oils and their excrement: the scent of outdoor semi-domestication. God screams: *Lost sheep are no good for my bottom line.* She is one of God's sheep. She's only semi-domesticated herself.

God told her to take the children. Told her to keep them safely chained to the wall, like lambs fated for sausage. Told her to mind her flock. To heed so many thousand non-sequitur messages. Told her not to speak of any of it to anyone. But she doesn't recall any of that. Her mind is locked in the ever-disconcerting present.

She hasn't spoken to another human, besides her two gaunt and spoiled children, for at least three years. She doesn't mutter under her breath. She doesn't write letters to her wealthy parents. She has no telephone. Food is delivered and left on her doorstep via automated services, and trash taken the same way. God rumbles again: *Coffee is gothic tea.* Everything God says feels important until she forgets it. She forgets what's said to her almost immediately, now that the hard tumor has invaded so much of her soft brain.

She cannot see out of her right eye. It's cloudy, blue-gray, bulging. Her left eye is brown and clear but still practically blind in the darkness. She has trouble finding places to set her feet. She stumbles. Cuts both palms open on the gravel. God snorts and snickers. *Earwax is no good for candles.*

Her father runs a law firm. Her mother runs on a treadmill. They send money in lieu of making visits. They smell like crisp dry-cleaning and new car interiors. They do not, did not, never will, know what to do about her. Their only child: a filthy lunatic. To them, she's two hundred pounds of lanolin-slicked shame, a PR nightmare. Someone best left to her own broken devices, where her oddness won't tarnish the family name further.

Through the combined magic of social stigma and direct deposits she lives in an asylum of her own design. She wonders how her mother thinks of her, if she worries about her, and if her father does at all. But Valerie does not wonder often. Hasn't for years. God won't allow her to take up self-pity as a hobby. *If I had your father's eyes, I'd make either cufflinks or soup.*

Her father represents the county water system and its many miles of corroded pipes that bring cursed water screaming through local faucets. He represents the land-owners who inherited land carved with miles of abandoned coalmines that leak acids and industrial residue into the water table. He makes sure everybody gets paid including the kids with three fingers and the kids with lumps where their skin should be smooth. And then Valerie spends the money he sends her on her water bill.

As a child, she happily drank water straight from the hose, before anybody knew any better. She was well behaved. Easy to look at. Exuberant under the appropriate circumstances. She was not born with three fingers on each hand, or three front teeth, or any of the other dishes served on the polluted water table. Her watermark was interior, hidden, tucked into her brain. And now, it shouted at her: *I'm offended I was not invited to this uncatered pity party.*

The voice she hears, like all voices we hear coming from between our ears, is an amalgamation. The scolding of teachers and mothers and television commercials. The soft coos of friends and kind teachers. Scraps of vocabulary stolen from every conversation and book she'd ever poked her nose into. That gristly lump of brain tissue, four hundred times denser than any healthy human mind, gave birth to a babbling God with a thousand parents.

She has a trick. She thinks, very quickly, between heartbeats, where her God cannot hear, *I am a beaver and this is my tree.* And so, she takes small messy, feisty bites, out of the tasks before her. *Snap. Snap. Snap. Spit. Snap. Snap. Snap. Spit.* A disturbing tic, even she understands that. But she does it anyway. With it, she can advance in paper-thin measures. She is slow but will topple whatever obstacle she faces with brittle teeth.

She's moved twelve feet in ten furious minutes. Both of her front teeth are vertically cracked, have been for years. Her bottom lip is scarred with the impression of her top teeth. She does not admit that her productivity trick causes her constant pain. She is determined to fell entire metaphorical forests, if she must. *Do you know how wicked swans are? They're dirty and they bite and they don't even wear pants.*

The sleet stings, feels almost hot on her skin. Her knuckles are stiff and white and chapped. The base of her skull is leaking valuable liquids. She reaches the edge of the fence that loops the train yard. In the dark, her fingers bounce across the chain links, searching for a dropped stitch in the knit. She was supposed to go to college. Major in business. Meet someone who fills out a suit well. And not have one blind eye and the voice of God shouting in her ear, *Don't get a cat, it'll eat your face while you sleep and steal your boyfriend.*

Her pets. The sheep: nameless. The girls: Amanda. Ruth. It was her calling, her duty, to sculpt them into ideal angels. To train them to want little and do all. To be grateful and patient and diligent and perfect. The girls her own parents never had, but always wanted. She had stolen them like a starving man steals day-old bread. It was no heavy crime; it was a divine mission. She remembers that children were somewhere on the property. She cannot recall their faces.

The wound high on her neck—what happened? A crow dropped a rock? A tree branch fell on her? A hobo attack? Doesn't matter. For whatever reason, she's bleeding wastefully. Blood and plasma dribble down her back, wetting her shirt all the way to the waistline. The tumor is weakened. Valerie feels lightheaded, adrift. The voice of God stutters, gasps. *I always wanted to be a tree when I grew up. Or maybe a spatula. A spatula is an elegant tool.*

A few steps away, the bottom of the chain link fence is rolled up like a wader's cuff. Her exit. She squirms under it, and rests there on her belly, weak and leaking. She carries no identification. She could be from anywhere. If the train yard workers find her, they'll assume she has traveled a long, tragic way to collapse in the wet Pennsylvania sleet in the middle of the night. No idea she lives just up the embankment, where a few dilapidated sheep are still attempting to outlive another winter.

Her mother told her, *Please, please, snap out of this. Behave. You can write whatever you want in your note-books, God this, God that, but please, pull yourself together in front of people.* And so, she did just that. Kept God's words to herself. She was not a bad child. Never wanted trouble. She always did as she was told. She's thirty-two, but still that child. She tries to respect authorities who hiss in her ear. *You'll never get clean if you dry off with a dirty towel.* She nods, and hopes she'll remember to wash the towels. She won't.

A flashlight lands on her hunched back. Footsteps on the gravel. The beep of a walkie-talkie. A bureaucratic voice: *Trespass, near the mid boxes. I'll hurry him along.* God giggles. *Spend twelve days fasting and you'll get high as a kite. Try it. You'll look great, too.* The train conductor shines a light toward the rolled-up corner of fence. *Get on out of here. Stop hopping rides.* They don't pay him enough to say more or linger any longer near a possibly dangerous vagrant. Hustling trespassers off company property isn't even part of his job description. As always, she will do as she is told. Valerie pulls her body onto the safe side of the property line. As the sound of footsteps recede, she stumbles sideways into brambles slick with frost and rot.

Legends told around small campfires warn teenagers not to go too far into the woods because of the Old Man of the Woods. He's the local Sasquatch/Yeti type who hangs out between the highways 51 and 22. The Old Man has antlers like a deer, the body of an ape, the musk of a dumpster on a warm day, and an appetite for road kill. Valerie's been mistaken for him on more than one occasion. So now the local boys have added details about the Old Man's big, teary eye: *blue as a dead baby's lips, they whisper into the campfire smoke as their girlfriends playfully punch them in the arm, and then snuggle closer.*

*She can't feel her toes. You know, sweat is just fat crying out for a time that you need to sit down with your manager and let him know that not only do you want a raise, but you deserve one two punches knock out a guy but you can't let him see you coming because the element of surprise parties who can't agree tends to be highly flammable but even—*Valerie bellows, *GOD, SHUT UP!* And to her shock, God does.

She's forgotten everything her God has ever told her. She has no idea, again, where she is. She blinks away more sleet. Her eye.

Something happened to my eye! It's been blind for years, but every few days she's shocked to discover that fact. She hasn't seen a doctor of any kind since she dropped out of high school to tend her sheep.

Her mother had wanted to take her for a second opinion, because the first psychiatrist she saw thought Valerie was faking, didn't believe the words of God were really rumbling in her ears. *This child is acting out. She's screaming for attention, but she can't bring herself to admit the cries are her own.* The prescription for anti-depressants didn't shut God up at all.

Valerie had come home from school a year after that diagnosis to find her mother sitting cross-legged on the floor, drinking vodka and pineapple juice out of a coffee mug and watching shows about wives who murder their husbands and get away with it.

You need a CAT scan, an allergy test, something! I don't know! But you need somebody to do more than ask you softball questions. Real doctors. Who can figure out why you're so crazy.

Mom, I'm not crazy.

Crazy people never think they're crazy, her mother sneered as she gulped her self-prescribed medicine, *I should know.*

Valerie hears a sheep bleat. That's one of hers. Isn't it? She knew she should go up and tend to it. It sounds hoarse, sickly. Her hands are all cut up, like she's been juggling knives drunk and blindfolded. And there's that pain at the back of her head, sharp and dull in uneven waves. She must have fallen. She tries to hold the thought. Maybe she tripped in the dark on a root or a bramble. She takes small bites out of the task at hand. Snap. Snap. Snap. Her bottom lip bleeds.

Sleepwalkers should never buy houses with stairs. God never told her anything helpful or uplifting. But the sheep, they had such wise faces. The others, the two dour girls who worked sometimes on the small farm, they did not possess the animal-optimism the sheep did. Valerie wondered how many sheep might be up there, if they had been fed lately, what their water situation was.

She never did go see another doctor. Didn't get a scan or even a perusal. There was no obvious need. She kept God's words to herself. She seemed fine, as if she'd stopped faking. The tumor stayed hidden as it grew. God kept babbling. She sucks blood from her lip as God warns her, *Don't turn back, you'll just get more lost. Hikers never see the same views on the way back and then they change their minds like rich men change wives.*

Before God started the constant yakking, Valerie read obituaries of other kids in Gour Borough who'd had brain tumors, terrible things that stole personalities and memories and the ability to talk without drooling. She would think, almost smugly, *I can't imagine losing my mind like that.*

Deep mud sucks the shoes off her feet. Her hood slips from her head. Her hair is short, crookedly shorn; the longest tuft is barely a centimeter long. She uses the same shears as she does on the sheep and girls. The buzzing clippers drown out God's voice and occasionally slice the top edges of her ears if she's not careful. She's nicked off slivers of cartilage at least a dozen times. She grits her worn teeth and pulls herself up the hill. Before she heard God, she was beautiful in the healthy, upper-middle-class way that effort-lessly intimidates poor kids with crooked teeth.

There are no campfires burning on her property to-night. No flocks of teenagers drinking warm beer and scaring each other with stories of train-hopping hoboes who kidnapped those two little girls eight years ago and sold them for parts. No gaggles of kids looking over their shoulders for the Old Man of the Woods and his big, dead eye.

The best cure for a hangover is three cloves of garlic, a bowl of strawberry Jell-O, and a call to your sponsor. God was never gone for long. She wished God would sing or whistle, but no, God just said stupid things, interrupting her and talking over her every thought. *I got my arm stuck in a vending machine once, but it grew back just fine, with hair and everything.*

She sees the flashlight beam of the train conductor between the sleet drops. She's halfway up her hill. A gun-shot bounces through the forest and the security guard's flashlight swings toward the sound. As of midnight, it's deer season. The deer have multiplied and thrived and nibbled away everything green they can get their velvet lips around. She snaps her teeth and plunges her hand into a bulge of slimy moss. She is climbing on all four limbs, delirious and hunchbacked, like a raccoon drunk on fermented trash.

She'd found the sheep farm for sale in the back of the newspaper. God told her, *Mind my flock, mind the gap, mind over matter!* Inspired that what God said somehow, miraculously, matched what she saw in front of her, she showed her parents the ad. She said instead of college, she'd work the farm and make her own way. She promised, with God on her side, that she would mind the flock. Her parents didn't know what else to say but yes. She'd be somewhere, doing something, talking to whatever lived in her brain, minding her own business and not interrupting their dinner parties with her wild eyes and nonsensical soliloquies anymore, not flunking out of yet another expensive school.

When she first moved onto the property, she could remember more. Her teeth weren't yet cracked. Her eye wasn't yet blind. She had twenty sheep, all healthy. Now, four huddled together at the top of the hill, stomping the bones of their fallen compatriots into the mud. If their matted, filthy wool had been sheared that year, their rows of ribs would be visible.

Her parents visited fairly often at first. They bought her furniture and light bulbs, groceries. They were relieved she was out of their house; dismayed at the one she was keeping for herself (her God was not a stickler about cleanliness or an expert on interior design). Her mother said she'd visit whenever Valerie wanted her to, but the words were said without enthusiasm, which negated the offer. They paid her bills but not visits. Valerie forgot about her parents, forgot her own family name. They had no idea their daughter had stolen the two girls whose faces they saw on every light pole.

Her father thought her ungrateful and pathetic. He took her school pictures down. Sneered as he told his wife he was disappointed in her childrearing efforts. Though she hadn't seen him in years, Valerie heard his voice on days when her God was most vengeful. *I'll give you something to cry about, sweetheart.*

She coughs. She stomps her feet to keep them from going numb. I hear the north coast of Nebraska is lovely this time of year, what with all the auroras on the menu. She nods and snaps her teeth. She could use a vacation. She could use a change of scenery. She's been staring at the same moldy walls for years now. She needs to get back to them, back inside them. That's where she's going. Isn't she? She's not sure.

The floodlight above the sheep's barn is always on. She's close enough for it to shove her shadow down the hill. She looks down, and sees footsteps, small ones, pointing away from the outbuilding. Bare feet in this weather. *What kind of wild people live in these woods?* she wonders. The kind the kids tells stories about. The kind they hope to not become.

When it tingles, that's how you know it's working. The ground shivers below her. A shallow earthquake. Deep underground, some long-abandoned mine tunnels collapse. Gravel falls from under tree roots into dark tributaries. Soil slips from inclines and settles in ravines. There have been dozens of these little rattles lately. The week before, one popped a jagged seam across her home's concrete foundation and tea-colored water began to trickle in. Valerie pulls open the rusty gate to her property. Her hands are as shaky as the ground.

Why are there sheep in her yard? Who put them there? Is this a prank? She puts her hands on her hips and whistles through her cracked teeth. She looks around for a camera crew, because this has to be one of those shows where an elaborate practical joke is caught on camera. Nobody's there but four emaciated sheep. She wipes drops of sleet from her eyebrows and trudges on.

The sheep are bunched together, shivering. Their diagonal pupils flex as they shift position in the light of the outbuilding. They assert nothing but their own presence. *Get out of here. Get. Go back to where you're supposed to be. Get out of my yard.* The four sheep slowly shuffle out into the darkness, steam rising from their chapped mouths. They begin to feast on the foliage they're now free to devour. Valerie's God has no comment.

She shrugs at that non-declaration and shuffles through the muddy yard to her door. It's locked. The wound at the top of her spine keeps bleeding. *Beauty's not in the object itself, it's in the upkeep. You'll spend more money washing that shirt than you spent buying it, if it's worth anything.*

She doesn't recall that the door on the other side of the building is wide open. She doesn't even recall there's a door on the other side of the building. She jiggles the doorknob again. *I like my watches to be waterproof so I can see what the time is while I'm drowning.* She's never broken into a house before, but her feet are so cold and her hands hurt so badly and she is soaked and her brain is leaking and people put sheep in her yard and somebody has to be inside to help her, and so she begins to bang on the door and sob for help.

She has an idea. There's a window right beside the door. It's not so high. She can climb through it. But she has to break it first. She peels off her wet coat and balls it around her fist. *If you want to change a life, change the channel!* Her wooly fist bounces off the glass without cracking it. She tries again. And again. *I have a prehensile tattletale.* On the ninth try, she cracks the outer pane of glass. On the eighteenth try, she cracks the inner pane. *Finches love human hair because it makes their nests so warm and soft.* After the fortieth punch, she's successfully broken into her own house.

While she's been out, the forest has come in through the forgotten open door. She's halfway through her kitchen window when the deer notices her, and she notices the deer. He's eating the cereal she poured into a bowl the day before and forgot to eat. He's one of the local specials: he's got three antlers instead of two, thanks to his seat at the head of the water table. Hunters are allowed to shoot his kind but not supposed to eat them. That's a crime akin to cannibalism: unpunishable because the evidence is eaten, but still potentially deadly.

She barks at him like a circus seal. Claps her chapped hands. The deer bolts up, his antlers puncturing the drywall of kitchen ceiling. His hooves knock dishes from shelves. He kicks over her table and the pile of trash and junk piled on top of it. He turns, and swings his antlers toward her living room. A lamp crashes and shatters. Another avalanche of trash tumbles from a moldy couch.

The deer bolts out the open door. Valerie struggles the rest of the way in through the window, and sits in her sink, white once, but stained iodine-brown from the unfiltered tap water. Shards of glass poke through her wet sweatpants into her thighs. *A fart is a burp that's been through hell.* She's been in this place before. It smells familiar. Not rotten, but not well. Sour, but not spoiled. Spoiled. Right. *Little girls are our economy's most fragile commodity.* Where are those children?

She hobbles toward the children's space in the house. The concrete block addition that was intended to be a garage. It's never warm. She's leaving muddy footprints in the mess the deer made. The door to their room is open. They'd last slept there three years ago, before she moved them to the barn with the sheep. *People with dentures are terrified of both corn on the cob and their imminent mortality.* She feels along the walls for light switches. The cots and shackles are empty. *One terrible part of divorce nobody ever talks about is mourning the children you two won't ever get to have.*

She has to get out of the house. *The tooth fairy carries needle-nose pliers and all the grudges in the world.* The people who live here could be back anytime. The people who live here, well, they seem dangerous. The place is a mess. There are shackles on the walls beside sweat-stained cots. They left the door wide open. *Tinted windows make picking your nose in the car politely possible.* But maybe they have a change of clothes she can borrow.

She's having trouble staying on her feet. She leans against a wall. The ceiling's green with some sort of mold. The carpet feels oily. Everything smells like sheep. She closes her eyes. Maybe she should just wait. Wait for someone to come home and find her. Yes. That's a decent plan. People are good. Well, sometimes, when it doesn't cost them anything. Whoever finds her will probably help her. Her neck leaves a gooey, bloody smear as she leans against the wall, then slides down to sit on the floor of the hallway she should recognize.

When she dreams, she sees her. God's always playing Ping-Pong. God looks like the girl Valerie loved in high school, the one with terrible posture but great taste in movies. She's smirking at Valerie with that sparkle in her eye that says, *When you're with me, you're allowed to have fun and be beautiful and eat every single fry on your plate.*

That girl married some thick and sturdy guy and had four thick and sturdy children. Valerie knows this because her mother told her. Not because her mother is particularly cruel, but because her mother had no idea Valerie had ever particularly loved anyone.

Sleet's dripping through the broken kitchen window and falling through the open side door. The ancient furnace can't keep up with December's winds. The house is cold. Frost forms on the mud on Valerie's socks. Her breathing is slow and steady.

God is great at Ping-Pong. God is sexy on roller skates. God knows all the best places to have a campfire and make-out and tell horrible stories and drink warm beer. God wears five earrings in each ear and had to retake algebra three times. God never meant to break her heart, *But things just happen, you know?* Valerie knows. It's the one thing she can't forget, because that message is in her bones, not her brain.

God flips her ponytail as she whips her paddle. God has red fingernails and jeans that are one size too small. God thinks subtitles are better than voice-overs. God smells like the cheap raspberry shampoo you can only buy at the dollar store. God drank the water too; God would have been so good at math if she hadn't. God would have left this town if there were a filter on her faucet. But things just happen, you know?

God has a plan. She's going to hop a train and get out of this town. She's going to go to Las Vegas and win a jackpot and buy a Cadillac and a round of drinks for everyone. She's going to change her name from Margret to Marley and she's going to learn how to operate a fork-lift for union wages and never, ever come back.

Valerie closes her eyes and remembers how the camp-fire was so warm and wonderful and she wishes she could never not feel this, the best feeling in the entire world, if only she could figure out why her head hurt so much and her eye felt so dry all the time. God whispers in her ear, *I'll bet you'd look great with short hair. Like, totally buzzed off.*

Another tremor rattles the train cars on the tracks in the yard. Sleet keeps falling. The water table keeps rising underfoot and hoof. Mines keep crumbling. A hunter shoots a three-antlered deer. Valerie dreams. The people who own the house will be coming back soon. She'll explain the window. She'll offer to pay for it. Things just happen, you know? *Have you heard about the Old Man of the Woods?* God asks, *Well, let me tell you. He has this big, dead eye.* Valerie punches God in the arm and snuggles closer, smitten.

04:00

Four in the Morning:

Paige

She hears the boys packing up their gear. They move loudly, even when they're trying to be quiet. She, like her brothers, is thick and sturdy. She, like her brothers, loves being outside in the cold and wet and wild. She, like her brothers, is not squeamish about gutting a fish or rabbit or deer while it's still warm. She, unlike her brothers, is still in bed, in the promising dark of the first day of deer season.

The boys are heading out to hunt with their father. Paige has not been invited along. She hears them quietly laughing and jostling each other as they lace up their boots and she seethes that she is the sibling they'd never even think to rival. She isn't one of them.

She's old enough. Her brothers went out hunting when *they* were twelve. She knows how to handle her rifle. Safety first, second, and third. She's a good tracker. She's patient and quiet and never not alert. *But the boys want their time together*, her mother had said. Her mother, who gave her brothers fluorescent yellow hunting jackets, and gave Paige a pink one: a shocking, sickening, pink one. Paige couldn't even pretend to like it.

She wants the day out, too. She wants to find a roost near a trail she'd been haunting. She wants to bag one of the freak bucks: one of the massive deer with three antlers. She wants to best her brothers, to have her father clap her on the shoulder and say, *Thatta girl*. She wants the whole family to eat her venison all winter and thank her for every bite.

She clasps her strange hands together. Three fingers and a thumb on each. No pinky fingers. She never took piano lessons. But her hands can handle a rifle better than her brothers, and they have all the fingers the other kids have. *Pinkies just get in the way*, she always thought. She listens as they clomp out to the truck, to open hunting season like the present it is.

She hears the doors creak open and then slam shut. She hears the old truck rumble. She hears it crunch the gravel with its rubber paws and sees the headlights slide across her ceiling. The house is quiet again, for a moment. She listens, hears everything. Her mother shuffles in her slippers across the kitchen to put the coffee on, three scoops of grounds instead of five: her mother is defensively frugal. The ancient coffee maker hisses and bubbles. She hears the television. The news. The weather. Updates on political hustling and grumbling. No traffic report yet. The sun hasn't kissed her continent yet.

She did not wear her pajamas to sleep. She's ready instead, in her camouflage pants with her folding knife in the hip pocket. She's wearing her stained, brown sweatshirt with the reflective cuffs, a hand-me-down that fits her better than any new, pastel things her mother hopes she'd want.

The reflective cuffs sparkle more respectably than gritty glitter on the ruffled shirts she's banished to her bottom drawer. She is further outfitted in wooly socks, hiking pants, and her thickest flannel. Her boots and gray-green cap are perched beside her bed. She slept like a firefighter: dressed and ready.

Paige's backpack is ready too. Box of ammunition. Bag of granola. Bottle of water. Flashlight with fresh batteries. Binoculars. It crouches by the closed door of her room, ready to be swung over her shoulder like the smooth, solid rifle that stands propped beside it. It's her older brother's hand-me-down twenty-two. She's snatched it and hid it from her mother in her closet where it waited to be her contraband sidekick, until today. She listens as her mother fumbles with the coffee, folds over unruly pages of damp newspaper.

Paige knows the place she wants to be. The woods between the old lodge and the new road: just south of Signal Hill Drive. There, a shallow culvert cleaves the tree line where twinkling, orange runoff water lures deer to drink. There, the sunlight doesn't filter all the way to the ground through the squat conifers and gnarled poplars. There, where the topsoil consists of crumbling clay that holds perfect hoof prints.

She knows the gloaming hours offer her the best chances to bring down the majestic buck she wants. She closes her eyes and sees him in her imaginary sight. She makes a fist with her right hand, squeezes it, watches him thrash in her mind's eye. Her gun isn't very powerful, so her aim has to be exactly right. A finishing shot once she gets closer, and then he'll be still and silent and hers. She'll get him, just like that.

She's been tracing the deer paths for weeks. Noticing the piles of scat, the broken twigs, those perfect hoof prints embossed in clay. She's been sneaking through the woods after school, when she's supposed to be at ballet class where the girls she hopes she'll never be assemble to contort precisely as they are told.

The lessons were a gift her mother had foregone a new coat to bestow: a gift Paige felt guilty for not wanting, for being repulsed by. Her grace does not express itself in motion, but in perception. Her power does not manifest as elegance, but as persistence. She is beautifully on her toes in heavy boots, not satin-ribboned slippers.

She knows her brothers and dad are not headed into the woods she'll explore. They'll head further north, into thicker woods. They plan to be gone for three days, sleeping in a musty tent suspended twelve feet in the air on the side of a thick tree, watching from their roost in shifts. They're taking a vacation, not undertaking a mission.

They plan to spend time together, sip the beer Mom didn't know they'd packed, and if lucky, snag a deer. Paige has no time for luck or lounging. She has to be home before her mother returns in the afternoon. Her mother shuffles across the hard floor, pours another mug of weak coffee, and loudly sighs.

Her mother will leave in an hour for her work at the diner. Her mother owns it, runs it, washes it, dries it, opens and closes it. The harder her mother works, the less money the diner generates. The old men who commune at the counter are losing the war with time. No younger men are coming to replace them. It's hard to find work in town anymore.

Paige hates the diner, with its flaking chrome edges and cracking plastic booth seats. Hates the way it smells like kitchen grease, stale coffee, and the yesterdays that felt more luminous than the tomorrows look to be. She hates the old guys who hover inside, the ones who look at her with wet mouths and greedy eyes, even when she wears her bulky, stained hand-me-down sweatshirt.

She hates that she's expected to respect the place and be polite and wear the apron and the tip-begging smile when she wants to hiss. She hates the way standing behind the counter for so many years has made her mother's ankles swell and shoulders droop. She hates knowing it will be her only inheritance. It is a small, collapsing space and she'd much rather have the whole world.

Everyone has the day off from school on the first day of deer season. Half the students would call in sick any-way if the district didn't make that allowance. Paige is expected to stay at home, to tidy up, to do some home-work, while her mother works and the boys all sit in a tree. She has no desire to meet that suffocating expectation.

She watches more headlights move across her ceiling: neighbors from down her twisting road heading out for the season. She kneads her hands together, excited, ready, impatient to join them. She knows she belongs out there, in the woods, between the brambles, where the deer with three antlers leave tracks.

And there are other strange things in her woods, things whispered about at slumber parties and around campfires. The Old Man of the Woods, part man, part ape, part elk, part apparition. Something like a Sasquatch who wandered East, but even more feral. Special to the land between the rivers, a legend she and her classmates could claim as their own. He is her school's mascot: a loner, a hero, a mutant who perfectly represents the remaining locals.

She's never seen him, just like she's never seen Santa or the Tooth Fairy or Jesus. She doesn't believe in any of them, not really. But some small, primal, faithful corner of her brain lights up when her eyes scan the raw dark and the static hum of rain strokes her ears.

And so silently, before she went to sleep, she prayed to anything that would listen, *Show me where the deer will be.* Paige knows the better half of prayer is work; she'd reconnoitered the lands, oiled her gun, and carefully packed that bag. She hopes she'll receive a sign once she steps between the trees.

Her father used to work at the gas station a block south of the diner, selling beer to the old men once they'd had their coffee. He'd sold lottery tickets and bags of chips and beef sticks and stale doughnuts and with his little paycheck, he bought little white pills to fend off his constant, unbearable pain. All because last year, he was playing Ping-Pong in the basement with mom and he threw out his back and couldn't put it right. Paige has trouble looking into his glazed eyes.

He hasn't sold a bag of chips in six months. His boss caught him asleep standing up behind the register and sent him home without his key. There've been five over-doses in Gour in the past year. Paige and her mom went to all the funerals, and she wasn't supposed to know why her mother cried so hard at every one of them. Today is the first day her dad's left the house in almost a month.

Ten years ago, the graduating class at the high school was over a hundred. This year, forty-three students are expected to scurry across the sticky gymnasium floor in polyester bathrobes and cardboard hats. Paige can't figure out why her family is still there, in the town with more empty, boarded-up houses than kids. She knows it's a ghost town, that she's one of the ghosts. Deer outnumber people five to one. Her odds are good, if she chooses the right numbers to look at.

She hopes it will be soon that her parents let the banks take the house, take the diner, let her mother sit instead of stand for a while. She hopes they'll move to a town with a pulse, a town big enough to hire both her parents and her three dopey brothers. But not too big of a town, and not too far away from her precious woods.

She hears her mother sniffling. Her mother only cries when she thinks no one can hear. When everyone is sup-posed to be asleep. When the shower is running. In her car in the driveway before she comes inside. Paige hears her mother turn the volume up on the television. A car commercial blares: a desperately confident voice offers no down payments on used vehicles that can take you away from wherever you are.

Paige wants to fill the freezer full of that fatty, gamey deer meat rich with flavor and heavy metals from the orange creek. Stock it until the lid almost doesn't close, until you can't see the bottom. Feed everyone until May. Her mouth waters and she smiles in the dark.

She wants to prove she's all the things the adults she knows are assumed to be but aren't. Strong. Steady. Brave. Trustworthy. She wants to be more of an adult than her father is, more of a force of nature than her brothers can ever hope to be. Be the provider her mother wants to be but doesn't seem to have the business savvy to become. A shield. A backup. A resource. She grits her crooked teeth.

She throws her covers back, hot with anticipation, too awake to lie still. She is jealous. Of her brothers who all have her dad's ruddy complexion and sense of entitlement and his affection. She flinches when she thinks of how he looks at her, like she doesn't belong, like she's not enough, like she's rotten all the way through.

There's something feral, uncivilized, offputtingly unladylike about her: everything. Her aunts whisper about it, loud enough that she can hear. Her mother sees it and looks quickly away. Her brothers taunt her and try to make her cry, but she never does. Her father just gives her that look of disgust and confusion and duty all tangled in a knot. In the mirror, she notices it and she gives her reflection a predator's smug smile.

She will stock that freezer. She will take aim and fire and bring home a buck with flesh that tastes wild and metallic and like victory. Her brothers will mumble their resentful *thank yous* between bites and feel weak and small and she will revel in her position at the top of the food chain, at the head of the table. She knows this, feels it like a truth not yet told.

Who fathered The Old Man of the Woods? Some colonial fur trapper, some cave dwelling ghost? And his mother? Some Appalachian forest spirit? Some trickster shape-shifter? Some creature conjured by the molds and lichens and worries that flood the valley? It doesn't matter. How you got to be yourself doesn't matter. It's only what you do with yourself that does. She can't wait to get out there.

She's practiced target shooting until she could pass as a military sniper. Learned to be a part of and separate from her surroundings simultaneously. Learned to watch and notice all the small things, the subtle shifts in language, in wind, in reaction, in attention, that signal danger or opportunity. She knows to hold her breath as she pulls the trigger, to exhale as her gun does the same. She hears her mother blow her nose and sigh over the droning of the television.

Paige remembers when she rose to her first fitting occasion. Two years ago, when Paige had just turned ten, she'd proven herself for the first time. Her mother was driving the old truck home when a big deer had dashed across the road, in the exact leaping posture the deer crossing signs always advertised. The more intense the circumstances, the more cleanly they expose true personalities from practiced, camouflaging behaviors.

She smiles sideways as she recalls what happened next. Paige didn't know if her mother had stomped on the brakes or if the deer's mass alone was enough to halt the pickup, but seconds later, the left headlight was out, the front bumper was dangling by a single bolt, and her mother had turned off the engine. Paige steadied her breathing and went to work.

The deer was thrashing on the road, his eyes white with terror, his body horribly distorted by the impact, wet ribs jutting into the wind at brutal angles. Paige's mother was shaking, gasping, her forehead resting on the steering wheel. The accident wasn't Paige's fault. But she was there, and she knew it fell to her to deal with the aftermath. She is still proud, recalling her composure.

While the television drones in the other room, each moment of memory is vivid in Paige's mind. She was calm, knew what to do, how to do it. Knew that her mom couldn't, wouldn't, do what needed to be done. Almost before the truck had come to a full stop, Paige was out the door. There was a muddy shovel in the back. It would do. Paige strode to the front of the truck with it over her shoulder. Stood between the deer and the single head-light's beam.

She didn't hesitate. She slammed down the shovel. Stopped the thrashing. Snapped off an antler. Stocked the freezer. And beamed toward the windshield, warm blood splashed across her chest. Her mother's been afraid of her ever since.

Paige sits up, stretches her arms. Leans forward, stretches her legs. She's getting ready to hunt, not to dance. She hasn't been to ballet lessons in six weeks. The class ends soon, and her mother will find out about her absences. Her mother's face will fall. Her mother's chin will quiver. Her mother will sigh, in that way she does when a customer sneaks out the door without paying.

Paige will not apologize. Her mother knows not to cross her.

Paige is smug, knowing her mother won't dare say anything to her about the dance lessons. It will be too late. The money will be already wasted. Paige intends to express no guilt, nor half-heartedly pretend to feel any. Paige told her mother she wasn't interested before the class even started. Her mother should have listened. Paige is tired of telling people what kind of person she is and not being believed.

She's exactly who she knows she is, out there, wandering the woods with her weapons and her wits. She is unseen, but in ways that benefit instead of belittle her. She moves smartly. Sees everything. Takes what she wants. This morning will be perfect, well, perfect except for the bright pink coat. She is nervous with energy she can't wait to expend.

Paige feels a rumbling. Like thunder coming from under the bed. The flimsy house creaks. The rusting pipes grind against their fittings. The rumbling only lasts a few seconds. Recent heavy rain is accelerating the crumbling of the abandoned coal mines that snake beneath Gour Borough like monumentally scaled, vacant ant colonies. She hears her mother get up from her decrepit recliner. The television gets muted or turned off. Her mother shouts down the hall, *Paige? Paige? Did you feel that? Are you okay?* Her mother sounds terrified. Paige quickly camouflages herself under the covers.

She hears her mother coming down the hallway. Sees her mother timidly open the door, letting in a sliver of yellow light. In it, Paige sees her mother's face: pale, start-led, worried. Paige's face is stoic, composed. Her voice is flat, emotionless. *I'm fine. We have a new sinkhole?* Her mother shivers at her assassin-cold response, nods her reply, says, *Probably, Honey,* and slowly closes the door.

Dogs and deer, they know when earthquakes and landslides are coming before the rumbling starts. They sense it. Maybe it's having four limbs against the ground. Maybe it's in their complicated ears. Maybe they know how to pay attention to danger in ways people, domesticated, insulated, and numb to nature, are simply out of practice with. Paige wishes she had their sensory acuity, hopes that she has absorbed some natural super-sensory abilities by spending so much time outside, submerged in nature.

She's jealous of the freedom of animals. Knows that some integral part of her is designed not for couches and recliners or swiveling office chairs, but for streams and meadows and forest floors. She wants to growl and snap, not chatter, not converse.

She longs to breathe air untouched by the perfumes of slippery detergents and oily plug-in air fresheners. The town she haunts, it's reclaiming itself from the invasion of people and their coal-extracting tools and descendants. Someday, it will return entirely to the wild energies that built it.

Her mother retakes her place before the crackling hearth that is the television. Paige creeps from her bed to the window above her small desk, once painted a pale purple but now picked to raw pine during her hours of time-out. She opens the narrow window. Sleet spits onto her desk and freckles her face. She happily inhales. She wants to build a home at the confluence of humanity and wildness, where rain is always welcome.

Wind sneaks through the bare branches and despite her layers of flannel and fleece, chills her. Not a lot of cover to hide behind, not this late in the year. The sluggish streams aren't yet frozen. The buzz of sleet will help to mask the noises of her movements and her deep, steady breaths. The day is still black. But the gloaming's gray approaches.

She knows the route she'll take. She'll avoid the roads, stay off the sidewalks. Hike around the town dump, not through it. She'll only have to cross a few lanes of traffic, and she'll move quickly. It's best she not be seen by any mammals: especially the two-footed type. The town is too small, and there's not much to do besides gossip about the lone little girl sneaking around with a gun.

Again, she imagines how it will happen. She'll spot him. Inhale. Size him up. Exhale. Aim delicately. Inhale. Take him down. Exhale. She'll hoist him up with rope. Bleed him dry with the blade in her pocket. Gut him efficiently and leave that for the turkey buzzards. And she will swing the body over her shoulders, let his head dangle over her heart. She will march home along the roads, triumphant, unafraid. The blood will stain her pink coat permanently. She'll wear it proudly then.

Ten minutes to five. Her mother calculates her leisure time to the minute. Time to shower. At six, she will be dressed and on her way to work. Paige hears the pipes gurgle. Tea-brown water falls haphazardly from the showerhead clogged with lime-scale. She smells the dollar-store shampoo her mother buys and dilutes to make it last longer. Soon she can hunt.

Paige will not become a woman like her mother. She will not domesticate herself. She will not weep every morning in the shower, where she thinks no one can hear it. She will not. Not all role models are positive and inspiring. Most are just image negatives of heroes.

She hopes her father isn't taking any pills while he's up in that tree, glugging beers with her brothers. She hopes her gentle, dim siblings will guide him safely home, letting him sleep in the back of the truck as the eldest navigates the bumpy roads home. She hopes her mother won't be up all night tending to him, after a long day at the collapsing diner. She knows that what she hopes for is the opposite of what is likely.

Just a few more minutes. And then, just a few more years. Soon, she can be truly free. She won't have to listen to the more polished but still impoverished girls who smell like complicated skincare regimens and whisper about her as she walks by, unwashed. *Wouldn't it be easier to just try?* her mother asked her that summer, saying with words what the girls do with their narrow-eyed sizing-up. Paige looked into her mother's exhausted, bloodshot eyes, and answered flatly: *No.*

In the future, she'll be a guide. Someone who takes tourists on trails. Someone who shows wealthy, urban types how to start campfires and pitch tents and forage for plump raspberries and mushrooms that aren't poisonous. She'd be a leader, if only for a weekend at a time, maybe even at the hunting lodge near the deer trails. And in her free time, she'd walk barefoot through any standing forest that will have her, where she can learn to sense the earth quiver before it shakes, to smell predators on the wind, to be more primate than person. She squeezes her narrow hands with hope, imagining that lovely future.

The other girls in the ballet class brag about skipping meals. They trade tips on how to feel full by drinking cold water and hot coffee. They examine themselves in the long mirrors and see only a mosaic of squishy flaws. Paige stands before the mirror on her closet door and sees only useful muscle and practiced skill. She is ready.

Three fingers on each hand is not a flaw. It's a gift. She can reach into tiny spaces. Tie knots with elegant speed. She can hold her gun more deftly than her father holds his, with his splay of meaty fingers. She holds up both of her hands before the mirror, proud, defiant. She is a lone huntress, was designed, destined, to be so. It is less of a sin, more of an honest assertion (to her at least), to defy society than it is to defy her own nature.

Paige hears her mother fumbling with a sticky closet door, groaning as she pulls her long, wet hair into a small, tight bun. Grumbling as she pulls on layers. Paige knows not to go into the hallway to say goodbye, to say something as banal and jarring as, *Have a good day, Mom.* Her mother's tired eyes are red and wet, not prepared for interaction. Paige is not cruel; she is simply focused.

Paige knows: when nobody expects anything from you, even the smallest accomplishment will be shocking. But because she knows herself so well, her accomplishments will come as no surprise to her. She is already the powerful person she sees in the mirror, the formidable person somehow invisible to everyone else. Because she believes in herself entirely, her eventual success feels utterly inevitable.

The front storm door rattles in its warped joists. Her mother's key turns in the crooked lock. The rusty truck with one good headlight and no front bumper hobbles out of the driveway. Paige shuts her window. Laces her boots. She hisses as she inserts herself into the neon pink jacket. Pulls on the backpack. Swings her locked rifle over her shoulder. Fits her headlamp onto her greasy forehead. All secure. All set. Out she goes, smiling with bared and hungry teeth.

Five in the Morning:

Marley

Not far from home, she pulls over to the side of the road and puts on her hazards. Gripping her phone so hard the glass might shatter, she prepares herself for what could be pivotal news. She only calls or emails the lawyer from her truck and when she's completely alone, when she knows nobody will see or hear or suspect anything at all. Her clunker is a confessional on wheels.

She's hired a divorce lawyer in another county. A county where nobody knows her. Or her husband. Or her kids. Her divorce lawyer knows things she can barely bring herself to admit in half a whisper. The lawyer is resolutely on her side because she pays him to be. The lawyer's like a therapist. Neither kind of confidante takes insurance.

The lawyer emailed: *We'll have a single addendum that adds, "and all other accounts in her name." Unless he knows about these accounts, and by your account (excuse my pun) he does not, this line should read like boilerplate and not at all like a loophole. I hope this sets your mind at ease in regard to your non-disclosed holdings.*

Marley reads that and feels both queasy and triumphant. She knows this lawyer is cheap and might be wrong, but she'll follow his lead because she likes where he's taking her. She also knows how her husband is with money: a sieve. When she was eighteen, when she met him, she opened a secret savings account. Just in case. For a rainy day. Because he didn't, wouldn't. Her windshield wipers scrape acid rain from glass.

At first, it was just a little savings account. But there was that time when the kids were so little, when she had that friend who wore unsensible shoes and pawnable jewelry. The friend who was a schoolteacher who mixed a drink she called "the teacher's assistant" that was just boxed wine and Smirnoff. And that wobbly friend told her about buying stocks online. Showed her how easy it was to set up an account. And Marley's secret grew from there.

She put five hundred dollars into a penny-stock vice fund: buying stakes in casinos and pharmaceuticals, in tobacco and alcohol companies, in rehab centers and gun manufacturers. She invested in the kind of industries that do better when people do worse. Her bones told her that was a good bet. Her upbringing and experience under-stood the concept of that fund. It looked like a risk on paper. A dumb gamble. A stupid secret to keep. But between the time her first child was potty-trained and her fourth child started middle school, that stock her bones told her to buy had split eight times. *It's just a little rainy-day fund*, she guiltily told herself. The sleet keeps falling.

She only checks the balance once or twice a month. And every time she does she feels light-headed. Today, her online brokerage account had a balance of six hundred forty-three thousand two hundred twelve dollars. The joint checking had thirty-eight bucks in it, and rent was due. Only when her husband's addiction became debilitating was she able to look at that balance and not shut her eyes and deny both family secrets.

But she has a plan. A good one. She'll sell fifty thou-sand worth of that stock. Say she won it with a scratch-off ticket. Then file for divorce on the condition that if he spent his half of that fifty-grand windfall on rehab, she'd give him her half too when he got out. He's never seen twenty-five thousand dollars in one place in his life. He'd go for it.

The kids all know about their dad and his pain medicine. *Medicine*, that wasn't quite the right word. The kids knew back and forth and sideways that their dad spent all day in his pajamas, in his chair, on those pills. The kids knew he'd sold the lawn mower and all their bikes. They knew he wasn't really looking for work. The kids knew that she knew, too. That last part stung the most. Marley's too nervous to put the truck back into drive.

The three boys were in high school already. The girl was soon to be. Marley had the first when she was only seventeen. Custody wouldn't be an issue, because he'd agree to rehab for the payout, and once he went there, no judge on earth would let him have those kids. It's a good plan, a smart plan. A plan that makes her hate herself for paying a lawyer to put it on expensive paper.

He'd worked at the failing gas station. She runs the failing diner. She'll lock the doors and never open for business again as soon as he signs on the lines, and she'll haul the kids out of town in time for school the next year. They'll rent a clean house in a clean zip code, maybe just up in Murrysville. They'll drink clean water that won't scramble their genes. Water that comes out of the taps clear, not weak-coffee-brown. They'll get braces and glasses and shoes that have logos other kids won't snicker at.

When they'd met, they both had plenty of options: ample, like their bodies. As time went on, those wells went dry, while the ground around them got soft and squishy and vile with acidic rainwater. She lost her office job. He lost his pension in a buyout. They scrambled to put generic food on the table with odd jobs and odder hours. And when even those odd jobs ended, they were demoted even further. Now she trades diner food for feeble tips and he aches and sits. They rent a crooked house that smells like greasy scalps and metal filings. Twenty years happened suddenly.

She doesn't love him any longer, she just can't. Pity, maybe, on one of those rare days she's feeling supremely charitable. When she was in high school, she told herself she was going to move to Las Vegas, buy herself a Cadillac. Learn to drive a forklift. Live in the sun. She hasn't given up on moving away. She hasn't given up on herself, not entirely or yet. Just on him. She can't unfurrow her eyebrows lately, and seeing herself in her rearview mirror unnerves her. *Who is that angry old woman?*

Curtis, their youngest boy, is a silly kid. Not that bright, but really good looking. He loves sports but is terrible at all of them. He'll be able to charm his way any where. All he needs are a few clean shirts and a decent school district. He'll bloom if she can repot him in good soil.

Austin, the middle boy, is a poet. He's all emotion and no logic, lucky to live in a time when he can be a carnivore but not a predator. Can't bear to look at a mouse-trap, even when it's empty. He just needs to be somewhere where someone will listen to him. Somewhere there were other delicate souls just like him, who would understand why he feels so much, so acutely. She hopes, for his sake, that his brothers miss at what they aim for on this trip.

Marcus is a densely built hassle. A fighter. An unsmart mouth that knows no form of censorship. He's a trouble-maker and pain in the ass. The kid has no love for any authority or boundary or limit. She loves him best because he's most like her. She'd been feisty once, too, before she'd been whittled down to almost nothing by her unrelentingly exhausting circumstances. She has to get him somewhere where his sharp edges can be polished, instead of ground away.

Paige is a terror. A heavy presence who has no fears or friends, a tiny, nimble assassin. Paige is why she'd cleared the house of knives and matches. Marley hopes that sly girl hasn't nicked a gun from one of her brothers to go hunting on her own, but knows she probably plans to.

There's a thick vein of cold, steely ore that runs through that child; that makes her more predator than princess. She needs a place with persistent, devoted, remarkably patient counselors. A place Marley can only hope exists.

Marley fumbled for twenty years to hold on to anything, to keep some kind of grip on the greasy wheels in front of her. But she was a sieve, too. Chances, children, her own husband: all clearly visible but too slippery to hold onto. They floated past her along lines of fate not parallel to her own. With this plan of hers, she'd be yanking hard on the reins, finally getting a defining vote in the direction her family traveled.

Marley replies to her lawyer: *Thank you! That's fantastic. When can we file the paperwork?* But it wasn't fantastic. It is officially sad. Her life, all their lives, would now be divided into before and after. Her hands are sweating in the cold as she presses SEND *and* begins the after.

She can't believe she let them go. The boys are all hunting with him. The first day of deer season. They all seemed excited to be together, if not excited to hunt. He's been clean for a week, maybe two? That's some-thing. They all wanted to go. Gave her their best, adorably pouty faces when they asked her permission. Curtis said he'd keep an eye on dad, put safety first, second, and third, the way they'd been taught. She can't believe she let them go.

When she met him, she was heavy and plain and boring. And so was he. On a scale of one to ten, on that oppressive, random, cruel scale, they were both barely fours. Still are. At best. She knows that. She understands who she is. Who he is. Was. Barely. But now? She has this investment. He has that addiction. So, what is she now? A six? Above average, in some way, maybe? She squeezes the steering wheel at ten and two. She's risen. He's fallen. Both levers yanked on by the same massive systems and legions of pulleys and gears.

And their kids? She will never say it aloud. Never admit it to anyone. But they're all fours, too. Barely. But if she spent her winnings on them? Could they be sixes? Above average by at least one or two measures? In the right light? On a good day? She feels terrible for even thinking about her kids in such cruel terms. But she can't help it. The world sizes everyone up. The world tells you what your real value is; your mom inflates it to make you feel better.

And she knows, even if she never says it, even if she never admits it, that if she acts like they're above average and puts them with other kids who are too, and spends money like they are, they really could be better—or at least able to pass as such. And that's the American dream, right? Going up one rung of the ladder at a time? Hoping the view from up there is worth the effort it took to climb?

She keeps her house in order by barking at her family like dogs. *Sit. Stay. Come here. Stop that. No. Good boy. Good girl.* She's so busy keeping things in order that she never has time to consider if the order she puts her house in makes any sense at all. Fed? Where they should be? Not shitting on the floor? That's all she can make sure happens. She realizes she's been sitting in the silent cold. She twists her key and the engine reluctantly turns over.

He was never a bad guy. Never angry. Never mean. But he isn't strong. He isn't safe. He's only half awake. Half there. He trusts her, so he doesn't have to trust him-self. It's not love: it's delegation of responsibility. Now he just sits in his chair, sweating like a cheese. He's become another job she doesn't get any kind of pay for.

And if he keeps doing what he's doing? He'll sink down to a zero. A less than zero. A drag on the whole familial equation. But once those papers are filed, the kids can climb a rung. Maybe, if she keeps them on the right trajectory, their kids, her grandkids, can be sevens. Eights even. Maybe. Someday. If. Her eyes follow the head-lights' beams across the forest. Hazard lights off, truck into drive: onward.

Her grandkids can go to college and learn how to ski. Her grand-kids can avoid the memories of nights without heat and light, of water so brown you have to unbrew it in a filter pitcher before you can drink it. Her grandkids will have braces and tutors and dogs that aren't mutts and hobbies that don't involve killing wild animals for sustenance and maybe they'll even ride on planes. Her grand-kids will take her out for sushi, and she will dare to try it with a smile.

But she doesn't know how to dream for more than the flashes of affluence she sees on television. Doesn't know the nuance, the detail, the how to be anyone other than a poor kid from the bottom of the shallow mountains of Gour Borough. She wants her kids to have a view, but she has no idea what that view looks like, what they might see from up on her shoulders, from one rung higher. She just hopes it'll be pretty.

Has she waited too long? Not long enough? When is the right time to blow up a household? How much is enough? Is it ever? Is the bribe she'll offer him enough? Her headlights turn the slender tree trunks gray. Under her tires, the gravel crunches like the num-bers in her head. She slams on the brakes before she kills the things that are standing in the middle of the road.

They're four-legged: that she can see. Sheep, goats, weird-look-ing dogs? One steps directly into the beam of her headlight. Yes, sheep. They're sheep—with coats that are overgrown and matted, with crusts of infection around their eyes. But those things are definitely sheep. And they're just standing there. She honks her horn. One of them tilts its head. None of them take a step.

Poor things. Oh, you poor little things. Somebody's been neglecting you. You just need to get cleaned up. Fed well. Looked after. You need to get somewhere safe. She knows what to do. She puts the truck into park and climbs out into the sleet. Then she grabs the muddy shovel from the bed of the truck, and steps toward them.

One by one, she nudges the sheep around to the back of her truck with the blade of the shovel, gently tapping each one on the hip. They do as instructed. *Come on now, yeah, that's the way.* She scoops them into the bed of the truck. At least they'll be out of the wet under the cap. They're lighter than she'd expected. Hungry too, no doubt. Sheep smell terrible. Her coat is a mess of excrement and lanolin now. She promises each one that she will do right by it. She's shaking when she gets back behind the wheel.

She has no idea what sheep eat. What they need. She has a big, empty shed. Her husband sold all his tools for a lot less than they were worth. There's room for this sketchy flock in there. She didn't know what children needed either. She figured *that* out. And if any of the kids give her crap about why she picked up the stupid sheep, well, then they don't yet know that love and guilt are different words for the same feeling.

The truck bounces over deep potholes. The diner regulars, they'll understand. *Just a few sheep in my truck. No big deal.* She hears a few feeble bleats through the window over her shoulder. *I know you're tired. I know. Oh, Honey, I know.* She'll keep the diner open through the breakfast hours, then shut it down and take her new babies home. If anybody asks why the diner's closed, she'll say it was a family emergency, and she won't be lying.

The yard at the house is fenced. There aren't any predators around. If there were, maybe there wouldn't be so many deer for her boys to aim at. She has shears and some kitchen scissors hidden in the basement where Paige can't get at them. She'll trim those sheep; get some straw for them if they want it. She doesn't know what a vet visit for four sheep will cost, and she honestly doesn't care. She'll make an appointment once the rest of the world wakes up. She realizes that that the freedom to spend money without needing to get an estimate up front must be what real wealth feels like.

She pulls up to the diner and parks her truck in the spot furthest from the door. Her arrival is as good as an open sign in the window. Her good old boys, as she calls them, will roll up soon. Five grizzled guys who once made steel beams and pipes and now make small talk and carbon dioxide. She knows more about them than their own wives do, how they feel useless and didn't understand how the value of a man could decline so much in a single generation. She wants to like them more than she does, but they don't realize how lucky they'd had it, as a group, and she resents their complaining.

Marley twists her tiny silver earrings. It was what she does when she's thinking: fiddle with the five posts in each ear, as if she could tune her brain like a guitar with invisible strings. She shouts at the back of her truck, *You guys can be tens, you know. Blue ribbon tens,* she pauses, and says quietly, *We're all tens, all of us, but things just happen, and we're just not judged real fair, you know?*

She unlocks the front door and flips on all the lights. The place is as she left it the night before: all the peeling corners and cracked pleather and broken tiles as clean as they can be, considering. She wants to think she'll miss the place, but knows she won't. It smells like bleach, diluted to the point it won't stain anything but will kill every germ it touches.

The woman who owned the diner before Marley traded it to her for an old Buick. The Buick ran better. And the Buick wasn't stuck on a highway frontage road in a town that didn't even have a mayor anymore. Marley got postcards from her sometimes. *Greetings from Destin, Florida!* She'd stuck the postcards to the front of the cash register with yellow tape and tried not to be jealous that she got the worse end of the transaction.

Marley yanks the mop out of the big orange bucket in the back of the restaurant and drops the bucket into the big sink. A gallon of hot water, a handful of soap, and a generous helping of elbow grease: it's a recipe for improving practically everything. The bucket gets rinsed and filled with cool water. Marley grabs a ladle and lugs the bucket out to her truck.

They lap greedily, splashing and bleating and shoving each other to get their tongues into the water. *Easy. Easy. Easy. Oh, Honey, take it easy.* She yanks the ladle back. She didn't filter the water. She always filters the water. Even scrappy sheep deserve that. Realizing her oversight, she snatches the bucket and dumps it out onto the gravel. *Sorry, guys. I'll be right back. Right back!* When she looks at houses for rent on the internet, she always shops upstream.

5:41

She stares at the water dripping through the filter. She wonders if she could get the kids to go to a church with her, once they move. She wonders if the kids will be okay, or if the deep wells of bad water have already wrinkled their genes and distorted the futures of her grand-kids. If an ancient philosopher's work can extend two thousand years into the future, then why wouldn't the work of a long-dead coal miner have the same reach and resonance? She thinks of her little girl and her three fingered hands. How many generations aren't going to be able to play piano in this valley?

She scrolls on her phone while the water drips. It's a high school reunion every day on that little screen. *Everybody trying to rub everybody else's faces in it,* she mumbles. It being the minor triumphs that look like major failure to anybody who managed to move away. Lots of posts asking, *Did anybody feel that earthquake? What hill slipped this time? What was that?* Marley doesn't answer. She never does. She knows what's going on and talking about it won't stop it. It's the acidification of the bedrock. It's responsible for the scary geo-hazards like landslides and sink-holes, what the insurance companies call mine subsidence and just won't cover.

She prefers anti-social media, like magazines and dictionaries. She searches for an answer to the question: *What do sheep eat?* Forbs, apparently. She then asks her phone: *What are forbs?* Oh. Weeds. She has plenty of those. He pawned the damn lawn mower.

Whatever took over where the grass used to be is waist high now, even after the frosts.

She puts some coffee on. Filtered water. Three scoops of cheap grounds instead of the recommended five. The old guys don't care. Her coffee tastes like broken crayons but it gets the job done: wakes them up just enough to remind them of all the things that make them angry, but doesn't rev them up enough to do anything about it.

The television goes on next. Always the local news in the mornings. The old guys think the bubbly weather girl (who's been doing the weather for fifteen years) should marry one of their underemployed, potbellied sons. Marley, with her body that's held four kids and her face that hasn't been unworried in almost twenty years: she's the same age as the woman who stands in front of the green screen and gestures at clouds. She wonders if, once she moves, she'll look any younger, if such a transformation could ever happen outside of fairy tales and advertisements for plastic surgeons.

Her phone rumbles: the lawyer has replied. He says that he'll bring the papers over before lunch. She can have her husband sign them whenever she's ready to have that conversation. The lawyer tells her to take her time, but not too much. This will be her husband's last hunting trip with the boys for a good, long while. She pours her-self a mug of watery coffee.

She twirls a pencil over her order pad, generates a to-do list for the day. Feed some old men. Shear some sick sheep. Bribe her husband to go to rehab and then sign divorce papers. Maybe do a load or two of laundry some-where in between. The coffee isn't strong enough for a list like that. There's a dusty bottle of whiskey in the back-storage room. That seems like a decent idea. It's the stuff you drink at wakes to toast a life that's over.

She stands at her counter and raises a small stained coffee mug with a chipped handle. *To,* and her mouth dangles open while she tries to formulate a proper toast. To vices, when you own them, instead of the other way around? To the peace that comes when you surrender? To feeding dirty kids? To *me,* she says, meaning all of that. The roof of her mouth burns and she feels like she deserves the sensation. All of the water for the sheep has filtered.

They deserve a drink too. Marley hauls the bucket out of the back-kitchen with her own throat still on fire.

From the dusty television above the diner counter, newscasters banter about the recent cluster of local land-slides. One of them is giggling. Another tells the viewing audience that there's nothing to worry about. The company that owns the station also owns a lot of the crumbling land it broadcasts to.

There's no cause for alarm.

But what about two 'larms? A wooden chuckle follows.

Are 'larms even in season right now? They cut to commercials.

She's afraid of the weather lately. She's Googled global warming and thinks it's kind of darkly funny that burning the coal that got dug out of her town helped the weather systems change, and now the resulting hard rain makes the coal mines flood and fall in. She vaguely knows the word karma, and thinks it probably applies.

She shakes her head and deliberately thinks of better things. Once she packs up her household, the landlord will probably board up the crooked, sagging house. Spray-paint red Xs on plywood they'll nail over the windows. The area's been attracting a terrible kind of tourist lately: arsonists. *All the woods are rotten around here*, she thinks, as she sips her mug without toasting to anything, *and the fire-setters are really just like termites, only faster.* The sheep gulp from her ladle.

She imagines her boys, setting up the sturdy tree stand, yanking the cords into place with shared strength. Aiming their scopes and bragging in advance about the bucks they'll down. She hopes her husband didn't stuff his pockets with his poison. Her hope is weak though, only one half a scoop of the recommended five. The sheep won't take turns at the ladle, so she puts the bucket into the back of the truck for them to share.

She opens her phone. Logs back into the brokerage app. It's still there. It's still monstrous. It's still hers. The sheep will get their own pen, a barn too. They'll have all the forbs they want, and bronze bells on thick leather collars. She doesn't dare wish any such luxuries for her-self, no bells, no whistles, no pedicures. That would mean she's high-maintenance. No, she *does* the maintenance. She will always cling to that martyr's pride. She shuffles back into the diner.

There's a pack of poster board and a box of permanent markers in the storeroom. She's had them for a few weeks, but hasn't been ready to use them. The purchase was a giddy, guilty one. But the paperwork will arrive today. The signs should go up tomorrow. She lays the art project across her counter, and writes, slowly, shakily, permanently: BUSINESS FOR SALE BY OWNER. She hopes she'll get half the price of the Buick.

She hides her signs under the counter. *Not yet. But soon.* The coffee maker and the running water have started to fog up the windows. She paces the diner, wiping away fog. Like all her chores, it's a job that's never really done. She wonders if she ever won't be tired.

She hopes the rehab place is nice: that the sheets are clean, and the rattraps are all outdoors. She hopes her husband eventually cries with antiseptic appreciation and writes her letters full of promises she knows he won't keep for long. She doesn't expect a happy ending, but she does expect him to make a half-hearted attempt at one, like she did.

The news returns with a traffic update. The parkway is backed up, as usual. That's her cue to flip on the ancient griddle. Her regulars keep time like Japanese trains, arriving at ten after six, every day. The griddle takes fifteen minutes to rev up. Everything takes time, always longer than she'd like. The sunlight is taking for-ever to gnaw through the fog this morning.

She'll go by Margaret again. She'll drop the pet name she thought was cool as a teenager. She'll be fully herself, as best she can. She'll give it her best try. Neglect doesn't stop eroding your heart once somebody puts a blanket around your shoulders. These things will take time. She'll shear those sheep, and in a season or two, they'll be beautiful. Money might not buy happiness, but hope? Hope it can make a down payment on.

A furnace instead of three space heaters. Five scoops in every pot of coffee. Name-brand cereal in the pantry. A computer at home instead of a library card. New jeans instead of knee patches.

She'll still rinse out and re-use plastic bags. She'll still buy dollar-store shampoo and dilute it to make it last longer. But her kids won't. They can have all the forbs they want.

The weather report includes a warning. Due to a week of constant sleet, the ground is super-saturated, and additional mudslides are all but certain. There's a broken water main in Mount Lebanon, and everybody needs to boil their water for a while. Politicians are calling each other criminals. The big hospital, UPMC Presbyterian Shadyside, will break ground on a new addition in the spring. Marley washes her hands with filmy tap water, knowing they'll never really be clean.

Six in the Morning:

Eileen

Her husband is reading the newspaper and commenting via a series of grunts and sighs on how profoundly, obviously stupid every living human is. That morning, he remembered his cufflinks but forgot his cholesterol medicine. Priorities.

She fills his coffee cup and splashes a little scalding java on the cuff of his shirt with a hateful flick when she sees the cufflinks, a gift from the one he promised he'd never see again. A brave move for her, out of character. He swears at her as she turns away. Her mouth is full of chewy, unspeakable words. He goes upstairs for a fresh shirt.

She perches a basket of laundry on her bony hip and shuffles down to the basement. She spends all day doing chores so he'll never have a fleck of lint to scold her about. Smuggled between the damp socks and dusty pajamas is a block of chocolate, a weapon she uses in retaliation for that treadmill he got her.

She hears three heavy thuds upstairs. He's clumsy with his anger now that he's old. Easier for her to evade now, too. She smiles with closed lips, and lets the chocolate dissolve into her bloodstream, amused he's decided to unleash his useless, floppy anger on inanimate objects for a change.

In the laundry room, she reaches into every pocket, hoping. Today: jackpot. Three crisp twenties, folded into each other, curved by the shape of his ass. She thinks she'll take the bills upstairs and hide them between pages of a romance novel, the kind of book she reads when she wants to remember what it feels like to be wanted.

She sorts the mail. Her child doesn't write anymore. She feels like she should have done more to tend the embers of that relationship, but she's not sure what she could have gotten away with. There's a flyer about CPR training at the Y. Eileen took that course after his first heart attack. She doesn't remember that much of it, and doesn't care to take the class again.

She hears a beastly groan coming from the master bed-room. He can be so dramatic. She sighs and trudges up the steps. Even though the cat died a year ago, she still watches where she places her feet, so as not to step on a crooked tail. She is gentle despite everything.

He's sprawled, shirtless, on the floor of the bedroom. His back to her, she sees that his skin is gray, like the fur on his shoulders, like bread mold. Last time, at the ER, they gave him a shot of something. Something that had to be given within minutes of a heart attack to be at all effective. Something she has in the medicine cabinet, just in case. Something she opts not to fetch.

He gurgles, desperate. She does careful reconnaissance in the doorway. She'd so wanted—no, needed—to get a new kitten after she'd been forced to put down her ancient confidante. He'd grunted, glared, and scoffed, vetoing her. She crosses her arms. She's been hoping for something like this to happen.

Sixty dollars buys a lot of chocolate. It's almost double her weekly allowance. She puts on her shoes, crookedly ties them. The Shop-N-Save, around the corner, just a block away. Open twenty-four hours. A non-suspicious morning errand. She needs something sweet, always has, always does. She'll get a receipt with the time stamped on it, a paper-thin but airtight alibi. Her mouth waters.

She smiles to nobody and everybody as she hurries down the still-dark street, like she's just out for an early walk, like all is well, and always has been. Like she's not moving though the horizontal December sleet without the benefit of a coat. Waves to the cars driving by. Are they her neighbors? She doesn't know. She doesn't get out much. She makes small talk with herself, *The rain sure is cold today, huh?* He's a partner at the law firm. He'd been a partner for decades. She wonders what that's worth, if it would be a lump sum, if they'll scratch his name off the letterhead.

She stands on the curb, shifting her weight from foot to foot, itching for the light to change. She rehearsed her lines in her head, in the shower, when she could playact the happiest ending possible. Shock, of course. She'd be so shocked, so saddened. *I, I just came home and found . . .* That would work. That would be just fine.

The grocery store doors open automatically, magically, welcoming her to a world of bright, warm commerce. The store contains more than she could want in a lifetime, and she feels like she owns it all already. Today, she can buy whatever she wants, as much as she wants, and nobody will say anything to her about it. Her secret feels warm and fluttery in her throat. Her shoes squish and squeak as she moves across the tile floor.

She will get a passport. She will go to Paris, New York, Toronto, be unworried. She will call her daughter. She hasn't called her daughter in years. She will take up tennis and oil painting and all the time and space she wants. She will get an impulsive haircut and a red-velvet heart-shaped box full of two pounds of milk chocolates with nougat and nuts. And, of course, a kitten. She realizes she is walking very quickly.

She stands nervously before a wall of candy. She plans to drink his whiskey. Drive his car. Smoke his cigars. Sell his golf clubs. Remodel his study. Delete his files. Flush his medicine. Donate his clothes. Track mud into his house. Rip down his curtains. Leave his couches on the curb. She will throw those cuff links into the little garbage can at the dog park three towns over. She buys the biggest box of chocolate on the shelf.

Walking to the register, she decides to only call his office, just his office, once it's official. They can call everyone else. That way, she only has to pretend to be upset once. She's been acting, pretending, to be so good and so quiet and so okay for so long. It's exhausting to never be off the stage. She uses the self-checkout stand, the robots they installed when the minimum wage threatened to rise. She takes her receipt, folds it neatly in half and slips it into her pocket. She skips through the empty parking lot, through the sleet.

Almost back at the house, she fumbles with her only key, the one that fits into the tacky faux-mahogany door. The house doesn't fit in Gour Borough. He has obnoxious taste, is a big fish in a murky, evaporating pond. She opens the door. He's still moaning. She thinks of her friend who had to put a hospital bed in the living room for her husband after his stroke. That woman changed filthy bags and sticky tubes and mucky sheets for three years and that house still smells and her friend is broke. She hurries inside, locks the door behind her, and takes a deep, steadying breath.

She puts the chocolate she just bought on the counter. She thinks about the time she found the receipt for the jewelry in the pocket of a pair of his dirty pants, and how he'd never spent even a quarter as much on anything for her. She never told him she'd found that slip of evidence. She unwraps the box of chocolate, throws the cellophane on the floor.

His phone is on the breakfast table. Out of his reach. Good. She sits down to unlace her shoes, and she listens to his feeble moaning. He liked to tell her she chewed like a cow. She smirks. *Who's making animal sounds now?* She holds as still as possible, listening for every audible detail. The furnace revs up, its white noise masking his guttural bellowing.

She slowly, quietly sneaks upstairs, peaks just one eye into the doorway. He hasn't moved, but he has shit himself, peed all over the floor. The moaning has ceased. She stands up straight and fills the doorway with her victorious posture. Hands on her hips, she calls his name. Nothing. Good. She calls him a worse name. Still nothing. Even better.

She stands silently, all senses scanning the scene for signs of life that aren't there. He was from a good family. He had connections. He was handsome. She would be fine, her mother told her before her wedding. She just shouldn't make him angry. And even if he wasn't perfect, even if he did have a temper, well, he couldn't be *that* bad. She hid the fact that he was behind concealer, foundation, blush, sunglasses, and when that wasn't enough, a tacky faux-mahogany door. She turns away, and wipes her eyes.

She goes to the basement to check on the wash in the machine. Still agitating. She paces the house. How long? She wants to be sure. She wants to be certain. Then she wants to call her daughter and apologize for her distance and silence and neglect over and over and over until her daughter believes her.

Her eyes go wide, pupils dilate. When is his first meeting? When will he be noticed missing? He starts his days so early. She scrambles to the kitchen, grabs his phone, unlocks it with his mistress' birthday. His calendar is empty until noon. Then lunch with *Her*. Gross. No business meetings until two. She has time. Yes, now, she has mountains of time.

How long has it been? Hours? It feels like hours. She creeps back upstairs. He is silent. Still gray. The room stinks. She's afraid to touch him, afraid to be sure. She runs back down the stairs, not carefully. She slips, grabs the banister with a sweaty hand. He always blamed the cat when anyone fell on those steps. It was never the cat.

That was close. Too close. Calm down. Deep breaths. You can't slip and fall and hit your head and die on the first day of the rest of your life. Get it together. It's going to be okay. This time I mean that. She nods. She grips the banister with both hands.

Her husband threw her against the wall when she talked back. He dragged her by the hair out of how many Christmas parties? Nobody ever stepped in to help. Just looked away, like it was impolite to offer salvation. And now she is alone with him, and there is nobody around to help that man. She wonders how many of the thousands of men who die of heart attacks every year had wives like her, who willfully fail to act on their CPR training.

No. No. Don't you blame yourself. There were all those little blue pills. He wasn't supposed to take them, not with his heart, but he did, because to him, it was worth it. He ate bacon. Drank booze. There were cigars after golf. She didn't stuff his brittle arteries with waxy plaque. He did this. She didn't do anything. Nobody can prove she did anything. She wanders, dazed, to the kitchen for her chocolates.

He might have taken one of those little blue tablets that morning. Before he planned to meet up with *her*. That's what killed him. Not guilt; he never felt guilt. Not shame; he never felt that either. And why would he? He was a pillar of the community. Nice wife.

A grown kid somewhere. Great house. Successful firm. High-five. Cheers. A great man, dead from suicide by boner. That's her story.

She sits at the kitchen table. Her heart is racing. Her jaw is wobbling. *Be patient. Be patient. Let it happen. Give it time.* She thinks of their only child, the daughter he disowned and cut her off from. The child's crime? Not keeping up appearances. Eileen gnaws her thumbnail, ruins her manicure.

Her fingers drum the countertop. *Now? Hopefully.* Back upstairs. She swallows and clenches her fists. She kneels beside him. He's warm, she thinks, for the first time ever. A pulse? She doesn't feel one, but she's not sure. *Give it time. Time will help. Time always helps.* She flees the room on all fours.

Back downstairs. She can't get her bearings. She vacuums the living room. Her daughter lives only three miles away. She runs a sheep farm, sells wool or sweaters or something. The daughter is kind of wacky, seriously religious. That always pissed him off. She bashes the legs of the gaudy furniture he liked so much with the vacuum, splintering wood.

She realizes she hasn't put in her teeth. Oh god. She'd gone to the store without her teeth. Scandalous. Old woman buying candy with no teeth at six in the morning: a public service announcement for dental floss. She shakes her head. She's worn dentures since her thirties. She brushed twice a day but he used closed fists. She vacuums harder, knocks over a lamp she's always hated, and stands perfectly still, listening to the sucking sound of the appliance.

Okay. Enough. Go up there. Be brave. Be sure. She marches up the stairs and looks him over with her shoulders back. She touches him. Not so warm. That's more like it. Eyes open, not blinking. Mouth open, tongue hanging. Looks good to her. Pulse? Nothing. *You're safe now.* The vacuum is still growling downstairs.

She returns to the kitchen and takes his phone in her tiny hands. A few more minutes. Don't call anyone yet. She cannot stop giggling. She is crying. She is shaking. She has never felt so much. His phone buzzes. A text. *See you soon.* She laughs harder. It took forty years, but she won.

She washes her face. Puts in her teeth. Turns off the vacuum. She has the phone. She thinks she's ready to do it. *Okay? No, but do it anyway.* Nine. One. One. Call. Barks like she's ordering pizza, *I'd like an ambulance, please.* She provides her name and address. She hangs up. Anxiously hurries back downstairs to wait for the authorities to roll around the corner to her house. Such a small town.

She'd wanted him dead. For her birthday, for Christ-mas, for her anniversary, for damn sure: that's all she ever wanted. Prayers answered, she sits by the door, looking around, imagining curtains that let in light, that don't have to be thick enough to hide secrets. She pictures a new sofa, a softer rug, a home instead of a house. She's practically purring.

She can't wait to call her daughter. She sends the girl money. She wants her to be happy. She didn't dare visit. He'd find out, somehow. He resented the hell out of their weird child, blamed her quirks on bad mothering. The doorbell. Garbage men in para-medic uniforms have come to take out the trash. *You're forty years late,* she wants to say.

She leads them to the man of the hour like a good hostess. No CPR. No need. She answers questions curtly, covers her face with her hands to hide the grin, feigning horror. It takes four paramed-ics to hoist him onto a stretcher. His gray face is covered with a sheet. She declines the offer to ride along with a shake of her head. On a happiness scale of one to ten, she is floating along at a four-teen.

His car. She'll have to take his car. She's never driven it. Not allowed. His keys, in his study? Right. Top drawer, on the left. On the desk is a huge raven, a black bird under a glass dome. His mis-tress stuffed it. She'll smash it with glee, crack all the feathers. And this room, it will be where she keeps the kitten's litter box.

The car doesn't fit her. Nothing of his world ever did. She nudges the seat forward. Up. Up some more. Moves the steering wheel down. Down some more. Fiddles with the mirrors. Ignites the engine. She will change all the radio stations to ones with happy pop songs about love and she will not feel cynical about the lyrics.

She puts the car in reverse, and with more horsepower than she has ever had at her disposal before, careens into the street. She backs over a shrub, hops the curb, and stomps the brakes. She doesn't know how to wield this inherited power yet. She shifts gears, moves forward. Deposits the car back in the garage at an angle.

The ambulance is only a few blocks ahead. It rolls patiently over the asphalt. No sirens. No red disco lights.

She realizes she doesn't recall where it's going. *Hospital? Coroner? Funeral home?* She must pretend to care, if only for a little longer. She will say she was too distraught to drive, that she was unable. But really, she just can't be bothered to follow him anymore.

The seats and steering wheel are leather: an interior skin. Supple, dyed black, long dead, evenly perforated, sewn into place. The seat is heated. Warm dead skin. Like she touched just minutes before. Skins like his taxidermist girlfriend works with. She will sell this horrible car. She slams the door and dashes back into her house. Yes. It's her house now.

Every time she blinks, she sees his open eyes. Recalls his dry tongue. Withers under his angry glare. Feels his Italian leather shoe bouncing off her ribs. Hears him say wrong things in a tone of righteousness. *Snap out of it. You earned it. You earned this. You did this yourself.* She decides to get two kittens.

Where is all the paperwork? What does his will look like? Did he remember his daughter in it? And insurance? How does that work? Who do I call? It will all work out. It will. Details aren't important. Not now. She will sign things people tell her to sign without reading them. It will be official and ideal, no matter what. She pops another milk chocolate truffle in her mouth.

Her dentures chatter. Her muscles twitch. She almost drops the next chocolate as she pries it from the box. His coffee has gone as cold as he is. She doesn't know what to do with herself, never did. She remodels every room in her head. She's not that old. She's young enough to live another life. Her next life will be bigger and freer, softer and brighter. She doesn't know what eventual forms those words will take but she likes the way they sound.

So many words in her head. Bouncing hollowly like the Ping-Pong balls her daughter used to play with. Relief? Guilt? Fear? Joy? Shame? Hope? Yes. All of it and more of everything. A ball of hot, vibrating static builds in the back of her throat. A lozenge of steel wool. A blur with hard edges. There is no singular word for this, she thinks, and so she screams into a sofa cushion. It's happening. This is really happening.

A gift basket. Fresh fruit. A bouquet of flowers. She'll take all that and his massive car out to her daughter's little farm. Her daughter will be relieved to hear the news. Hopefully be happy, or at least not furious, to see her. *I didn't want to leave you. I am so sorry I haven't called. You look lovely.* She knows her daughter will look lovely. *I love you, Valerie. Always have. Just not the way I wanted to.*

He settled all those lawsuits with all those people about the water issue. He always handled the cases about the water, paid people to be quiet and not complain. He told them it was safe, it was fine, nothing was proven, that stuff from the taps is perfectly safe, even if it smells a little funny, even if it's not perfectly clear. They drank bottled water in their house. If she was a fraud when she smiled and said she was fine, well, she learned from the best.

The quiet of her house is spooky. She turns on the television to override the silence. The news tells her diplomats are talking, celebrities are divorcing, the heavy rains are triggering sinkholes and mudslides, and the precipitation will continue to be histori-cally severe for the foreseeable future. She wiggles her toes in her shoes. She gets up to move her legs. She walks out the door.

To Eileen, it is an objectively beautiful day, the temperature hovering around freezing, the barely-morning sky dark gray with stinging sleet. She remembers the laundry. She should check on it when she gets back. She will put the wash into the dryer. She will have another piece of chocolate. She will draw a hot bath and drink cold wine. She reminds herself to breathe.

The phone call. The one she still has to make. His office. She almost drops the phone getting it out of her pocket. She stops pre-tending and speaks the truth. *Hello? Hi. This is Eileen. Herbert died. Not sure how you want to handle that. Me? I'm great. Never been better. Why wouldn't I be?* The receptionist incorrectly assumes her terseness is a manifestation of shock.

She could have run. Taken her daughter and fled. She could have spoken up. Called an authority bigger than him. Said something. Tried. It was never the right time. He had guns in his study. He never went hunting out-doors. He had an axe in the garage. They don't have a fireplace. Who would believe her? It was never quite bad enough. She was never sure of anything. She opens his text messages and tells his mistress, *I died so our lunch date is canceled.* She smiles. She really did win.

Every footstep, a syllable: *Freedom. Inhale. Sleep well. Exhale. Relax. Lightness. You're fine. Okay.* She is skipping like a child. Fast and nimble and farther away from the past and the aches and pains and silence. His ashes will get flushed. She will use his urn as a candy dish. Keep it on the kitchen counter. Keep it full.

His phone buzzes in her pocket. His office. *Yes? At the hospital. The coroner's. I don't know. It just happened. They're doing whatever it is they do to a dead thing. Yes. A thing. He's just a thing. Always has been. Don't pretend you didn't notice.* The voice on the other end is patronizingly understanding of her tone. She doesn't know if it's one of the partners or a secretary. It doesn't matter. Nobody can prove she did anything, because she didn't.

She walks past a half-dozen houses with crooked front stoops and moldy awnings. Steps over sidewalks full of cracks. Nobody lives here anymore. There used to be kids here. Out on bikes. Running in sprinklers. Trick-or-treating. Then that girl disappeared and people got wary of each other, and the town slid faster downhill. She will give his Steelers season tickets to the Boys and Girls Club in this town, if there's still a Boys and Girls Club in this town. There's so much she doesn't know.

She has her wallet. Forty dollars left of the laundry money, plus her weekly allowance. She wonders what he made, what his salary is, what the mortgage is, or if it's paid off like damaged water-drinkers he paid to keep quiet. She takes off her small, golden wedding band and flicks it into the street. Naughty girl: no sense of values.

The phone. Unknown numbers. She doesn't want to talk to any of them. She squeezes it, turns it off. Clouds drift. Time ticks. Lights change from green to red and back again. Nothing and everything is different. She hears a gunshot boom from somewhere in the hill behind the train depot. *You kill it, you eat it.* People do what they can to survive.

He was dead, wasn't he? He was. They put a sheet over him, over his face. He was cool. Gray. Eyes were open. He was. He was. The ambulance didn't turn on its lights. Don't worry. He won't come back. This isn't a horror movie. She's gone all the way around the block. Her house is right in front of her again. Her feet fall in time with the words she repeats in her head, *He was. He was. He was.*

The garage door is still open. The bedroom carpet is stained. The car is parked crookedly. The laundry is done. And the chocolate won't taste as good, now that it's not forbidden. Everything will fall into place. One thing at a time. But first things first: she plucks the axe from its hook in the garage, and marches inside to destroy the treadmill.

Seven in the Morning:

Tasha

She feels sedimentary while watching television and working her immersively dull jobs. Igneous while arguing and singing karaoke. Metamorphic while studying geological information. Artificial while hiding her irritations behind a customer-facing smile. Tasha is running the ovens and register at a strip-mall bakery, making warm cookies for cold housewives. But in her heart, she's a geologist.

She wears a Fordite pendant around her neck. It's made of layer upon layer of automotive paint, baked into an agate-like material on the floors of Detroit auto plants, and polished on a lathe until it gleams. It represents humanity better than anything Tasha has ever seen. It's waste made into treasure.

She makes minimum wage forging dough into cookies, a minor metamorphic process. She has her master's in geology and is working at the bakery until she begins her PhD in the fall. The lack of openings in her field frightens her, makes her afraid that her curious brain might be a fatal liability. When she applied to the bakery, she only listed her high school diploma, and spoke with simple words during her interview.

If the funding for just a few of the dozens of geologically-influenced and long put off infrastructure projects around Pittsburgh were available, she and her mentor could have been rebuilding the fragile city instead of serving cookies and beers in its suburbs. She was furious she hadn't been hired to get to work, doing remediation on abandoned coal mines that gurgled acid from below or structural reinforcement on the bridges that dropped concrete from above. She burns two-dozen chocolate chip cookies while reading a paper on local geohazards. She pulls the tray of blackened dough from the oven and curses under her breath.

Trying not to think about the slow march of geological time versus the swift avalanche of shoddy human decision-making is difficult: especially when pale suburban women came in to pick up orders. They either avoid eye contact or try to be overly friendly with her. She senses that both reactions were expressions of some amalgamation of racism and classism, words she doesn't dare utter in an area full of poor white people.

She knows how prone to slope instability the hillsides around here are. And now, with this rain that's been falling for weeks? And the accelerated rock acidification? And the hundreds of abandoned mine lands lurking under everything? Landslides and sinkholes are utterly inevitable. She'd texted her mentor: *We told them AGAIN about the low shear rock strength last fall!!!!!* She sighs as she reads about sinkholes that bloom like dandelions. The Appalachian Mountains were higher than the Alps a million years ago. They're not going to stop eroding any time soon.

She's too opinionated. Too uptight. Not any fun. Basically, she dares the world to take her seriously. *The world doesn't revolve around you, Tasha,* her mother would scold. Tasha would shoot back, *I have my own gravity.* Their diametrically opposed and equally valid points did not cancel each other out.

When her mentor, who's now working in a dingy underground pit changing oil on late-model cars, texted her to come to the seismic lab, to see just the constellation of recent, subtle seismic activity triggered by the heavy rain, she angrily replies that she can't go. Even though the curiosity is eating her alive. She's playing the long game. Playing to win. She needs every hour at every one of her three minimum wage gigs. Every dime.

She knows how rich people get that way. Over generations, not paychecks. So she budgets according to time. One bucket for grandchildren. One bucket for now. One bucket for her own future. She is going to build a legacy, one fake smile, one warm cookie, one published paper on the geological underpinnings of Appalachian Plateau, at a time. If she invests a third of her money for people born a hundred years after her death, they'll name all their babies after her. Even the boys.

She's obsessed with landfills. How the pressure exerted on tons upon tons of trash might create new materials over time, how trash could become, if not treasure, then at least a new kind of interesting flake in the earth's crust, how man-made materials and activities could be catalysts for geological metamorphoses. She turns on the mixer and adds raisins to a wad of dough.

Layer upon layer. Year upon year. *Thank you! And you have an excellent day!* Another five-dollar bill flutters into her tip jar. Another layer of silt for her grandchildren to build their lives on. *You are so welcome. See you soon!*

A tired looking woman dressed all in gray wanders into the store. Tasha gives burnt or otherwise imperfect goods to the sketchy looking people who came in looking for a bathroom. It moves them along, gets them back out the door. A loitering, unwashed person was like an anti-advertisement to the better-off clientele. Bad for tips. Bad for her long game. Tasha eyes the cookies she'd burnt earlier. Yes, she quickly judges others with her eyes. Everyone does.

The woman had driven up in an old, angular Celica with—what was that? A coffin? Strapped to the roof. What a day. Seismic clusters. Goth ladies hauling coffins in the rain. Never a dull moment in Westmoreland County. Tasha sighs. It's always *something*.

The woman stands at the counter, looking confused.

Can I help you?

Just a cookie.

What kind?

Um, the biggest one.

One of those days?

The woman stares at Tasha. Tasha procures a snickerdoodle. The woman approves.

Before Tasha can hand it over, the woman blurts, *I found out my boyfriend died. Got a weird text, called his office, and they told me that yeah, he died. This morning. Died. We were supposed to have lunch. And, oh, oh my god, I feel like an asshole because I'm, I'm just so very, very relieved.* Tasha understands. When her last boyfriend had told her she was *just too intense, he couldn't, like compete,* she'd been relieved too, proud, almost. Tasha glances out of the front window, into the parking lot—and gets scared.

She points with a straight arm to the parking lot, *Tell me he is not in that box on your car.*

What? No! That's just—that's something else.

Oh?

It's mail I have to drop off.

Really?

The woman smiles with her eyes but not her mouth, *He would never have fit in that little box.*

Tasha hands over the cookie, *Okay. In that case, this'll be three forty-five.*

The woman gives her a five and stuffs the change into the tip jar.

While the woman nibbles the edges of her cookie, Tasha offers, *I'm sorry about your boyfriend.*

I think he's my ex now?

Maybe former is the right word?

Yeah. That sounds better.

Well, I'm sorry about him.

At least somebody is.

The women smirk at each other.

Can I ask what's in the box though?

It's a costume. A hyper-believable monster costume. I make and sell stuff like that.

Halloween?

I think it's a sex thing. The buyer's anonymous. Won't even tell their address. I have to leave it at the drop-shipping place next door with just an account number.

Interesting.

Rich people are into all sorts of weird stuff.

Yeah. They really are.

Tasha wipes down the counter and then turns to pull another dozen cookies out of the oven. Bake by ten, sell by four. A short game.

She flicks the hot cookies onto a cooling rack and thinks about rings on trees and petrification and geodes and mosquitoes locked in amber and caves full of fragile crystals. She closes her eyes and imagines how stones form over eons in the absolute dark. How the trash she takes out today will someday form some new artifact of humanity embedded in the ever-eroding Appalachians.

Tasha assumes that in the future, rich people, if humanity manages to survive this geological era, will someday measure that material by the carat and facet it until it glows and set it into claws of gold. Maybe her descendants will give each other those stones as gifts. Rich people are into all sorts of weird stuff.

Chemistry and physics plus time equal geology. Time is the greatest variable in the equation. Time changes everything. Nothing is truly inert if you give it enough time, she thinks. Add enough time to geology and you get astronomy. Tasha watches an expensive car idle at the stoplight outside. *That driver and I are made of the same busy star-exhaust.*

7:21

What's that? The non-grieving non-widow asks. Tasha didn't realize she'd said anything out loud.

Oh. I said that driver and I: we're made of the same star-exhaust.

You're deep.

No, I've never even dug into the mantle.

The woman looks perplexed, but doesn't ask her to explain. People only ask for clarification of mumbling when the subject of the mumbling might be them.

Tasha has not told her family that she's been accepted into the PhD program. Does not tell them how she's almost already paid off her other student loans. She doesn't mention the fascinating theoretical books she reads, or the journals she's been published in. *You make your little brothers feel bad, bragging like that.* They do know that she works three jobs for minimum wages, and they think that after all her big words and fancy schooling, she got what she deserved.

She loses herself in thoughts of generational time, where she fits into the string of beads that is her family history. Farmer. Merchant. Slave. Slave. Slave. Slave. Soldier. Maid. Elevator operator.

Street sweeper. Bus driver. Geologist. Every body just one more layer of sediment, crushed together by time. Heat forces dough to become cookies, and the chemical changes smell comforting.

The woman throws her napkin into the trash, destining it to become some new form of covetable stone in a few hundred thousand years, waves goodbye to her single-serving friend, and leaves the store. The bell jingles. Tasha's alone in the shop.

Tasha knows she's just one of nine billion people to ever stroll the crust of the earth. No, ten billion, she thinks, considering her pre-human ancestors. She's not proud, no, the opposite. Humbled by the scale of things beyond herself. A volcano is a pimple on the earth: it's only catastrophic to the relatively microscopic creatures that scurry in its shadow. *We're all one geological hiccup away from disaster.* She wipes down the table where the coffin-hauler sat.

Maybe there'll be an increase in infrastructure spending soon. Noticeable events always trigger funding: and these landslides and sinkholes? They're fairly small, but they're making the news. Maybe she can get her research going. Join a big lab. Discover or engineer a new form of stone. Maybe. In the meantime, that oatmeal raisin dough needs to finish baking. She watches the woman wheel the coffin on a dolly into the drop-shipping place.

Every year, several million earthquakes rattle the earth. Most are too small to be felt. But they're happening constantly, under every foot and claw and root. Continents move like slow-motion jigsaw puzzle pieces. Mountains slip. Underground caves close in on them-selves. Tasha arranges more dough on a sheet, knowing the balls will flatten as they absorb heat.

She goes to her next job at three. The old hunting lodge. She does housekeeping. Folds towels. Changes sheets. Wipes out showers. It's not a terrible job. Less human interaction, unless one of the guests walks out of the shower without a towel. Tasha laughs at the men who pull that stunt. The other housekeeping girl, Alice, cries when it happens. Tasha envies that girl's ability to still feel things. Tasha's discipline has flattened her emotional sine wave. She watches the woman drive away in her now coffinless car, and genuinely hopes that she has a good day.

She's daydreaming about fellowships and hyper-sensitive monumentally expensive seismic machinery when the window shatters. She dives to the floor. Glass in her hair. Eyes shut. Ears ringing. She's okay. Nothing hurts. Glass everywhere. She peeks through the display case. Sees three guys in hunting gear running toward the shop. It's always *something.*

They're teenagers. Gangly. Pimply. Pale. They shout over each other.

Oh my god. Oh my god. Curtis, you dumbass.

I'm sorry. I'm sorry.

Is anybody hurt?

Anybody here?

Oh my god.

How could you do that?

An accident! An accident!

So much for safety first, second, and third.

I'm sorry. I'm sorry.

You suck at driving, Curtis.

I'm real scared.

Tasha stays where she is. It's hunting season. Isn't it? They're kids. Just kids. They're freaking out. One of them drove a truck through a shop window. They're as stunned as she is. It's not a robbery. It was an accident. An accident. She pulls her phone from her pocket. Call somebody. The fire department. Emergency. Nine. One. One. Call. *Hello?*

What is your emergency?

Uh, car accident? No one's hurt. I mean, I don't think. Lots of broken glass. At Astrid's Bakery, south of Monroe-ville, near Gour, off Twenty-Two, next to the Drop Shop, you know, the bakery next to the mailbox store, She keeps talking and is surprised at how clear and unaccented her voice sounds, like a broadcast journalist, like someone who professionally projects gravity.

The boys try to follow her one-sided conversation. One shouts, *An ambulance. Our dad. He needs an ambulance.*

An ambulance, she repeats, hoping the voice on the other end will dutifully upgrade the urgency of response. The dispatcher ends the call after promising her that help is en route, but to stay on the line. Tasha stands up, brushes sparkly bits of glass from her shoulders. The three boys are shaking. One steps through the broken window and reaches a long arm out for her phone, *Let me talk!* She gives it to him.

The oldest, or, at least, she thinks he's the oldest—he's the tallest and broadest of the boys, begins explaining in a tone far more discombobulated than her own, *When we were out hunting. Well. No phone battery. Curtis forgot the charger. Dad took too many pills. Yes. I don't know. They're little and white? Nodding. Yes. I don't know. I don't know how many. Enough? We got him into the back of the truck. To get help. No service out there. We just drove. First place we could. He's in the back of the truck. No. Yes. No. Conscious? I don't think he is. Curtis! Is he breathing?*

Curtis says no.

It all feels like slow motion. The boys are in the bed of the pick-up truck. Tasha sees a muddy boot sticking out of the back. They're crying, jostling each other. One is trying to do CPR on the body wearing the boot. One waves in a roaring ambulance like a scarecrow. Paramedics flow from the back of the van like navy water. Tasha watches the flashing red lights sparkle on the shards of glass.

Traffic slows around the bakery. Rubberneckers. The boys are now out of the truck, arms around each other. Tears. Howls. Tasha is still behind the counter. She is quite aware that she's an extra on the set of an unfolding family emergency and tries not to stare at the unmoving boot in the back of the truck. She watches the cars slowing down, gawking at the gawkers. Hopes that staying out of the way is kind of functional help. Now police arrive.

Nodding. The boy said nodding. That's a heroin thing. White-people crack. Poor people are into some weird stuff, too. Their dad. She should do something. She doesn't know what. A police officer with a pink face is collecting the boys' hunting rifles. Puts their guns in the trunk of the cruiser. Takes some notes. Pats them each on the shoulder. The officer looks at her, standing there in the bakery. He motions her to stay where she is.

A cot. The paramedics. They're lashing the dad to a cot. They're not doing CPR anymore. It must have been too late a while ago. Heads shake. Faces look down. The cot rolls into the ambulance. The oldest boy climbs in after it, loyal like a dog. Doors slam. The two other boys sink into the back of the police car like it's a taxi. The ambulance leaves. The police car follows. A great rum-bling and then a sudden silence: an event like an earth-quake.

She's still standing behind the counter. No statement given. No questions asked. Like she wasn't even there. She takes a deep breath. Picks the glass out of the tip jar and empties the coins into her purse. Steps carefully to the door and flips the neon sign on it from open to closed. There's a Ford F150 where the tables are supposed to be. The hood is still warm, turning fallen sleet to steam.

A broom. Yes. A dustpan. Yes. She's on the clock. Time hasn't sped back up yet. Her ears are still ringing. Sweep. Then mop. She writes down the license plate number because that seems like something she should do, even though the truck isn't going any-where. Her boss will need it for insurance. Probably. She has no idea how that sort of thing works. She's a geologist, not an insur-ance adjuster.

Her boss. She should call. But sweep first. *One thing at a time. Move carefully. Like a glacier, not an avalanche. Long game. Mind your steps.* No. Her phone! That kid has her phone. She scowls. Time returns to normal speed. *That kid stole my damn phone.* She drops the broom. She stomps to the back room and calls the shop owner from the landline.

The woman who owns the bakery is almost sixty and she's never had a black friend, and she's careful to be technically friendly to Tasha.

Hi there! What's cookin'?

Astrid, there was, an incident, I guess would be the best word? A kid whose dad was overdosing drove a truck through your front window. I'm sweeping up the glass.

My god.

I'm okay though.

Okay. I'll be there as soon as I can. I mean, if you think it's safe?

It's safe enough.

The glass fills a trashcan. Blue edges. Glittering dust. People die all the time. Are born all the time. Stars are forming. Collapsing. Tectonic plates shift. Tunnels and coalmines and pyramids fall in on themselves. The universe expands. This wasn't unusual. She was just there to see it. That's the unusual part: that anybody's alive in the first place to witness anything. Draw a line a mile long to represent the lifespan of the universe and only the last eighth of an inch of it is how long there's been life on Earth. She learned that as an undergrad.

Some shards still cling to the edges of the window frame. She knocks them loose with the broom handle. She wants the place to look as normal as possible. Like nothing happened. Like it's a typical day at the bakery. But it's not. Is it ever? No. It's always *something*. Time doesn't stop. The universe keeps expanding.

She wonders if one of the boys will bring her phone back. If she'll have to pick it up from the station or hospital or wherever it went. Wonders if one of the grieving boys will scroll through her photos and notice that she has a thousand pictures of cracked geodes and sinkholed landscapes, but very few pictures of friends.

Tasha's mentor texts her a bit of trivia. The phone rumbles in a dirty denim pocket. *The seismic lab has picked up eighteen local tremors in the last twenty-four hours. 18!!!!* The oldest boy reads the message. He realizes he's shaking too. He puts Tasha's phone away and looks out the window of the police cruiser, but he doesn't see anything but his dad's slackened face. He's afraid to call his mom; he doesn't know what he will tell her.

Tasha fills the mop bucket with scalding, tea-colored tap water. She'll have to throw out anything that might have glass in it. All the dough in the mixer. All the cookies on the cooling racks. Wipe down everything. Be careful. Don't want anyone swallowing glass. Don't want anyone swallowing anything so dangerous an ambulance gets summoned to the bakery again. Landfills will swallow everything instead.

A coffin-shaped box with a costume inside it. An empty shell where a soul's supposed to fit. She stops. Is she thinking about the body in the ambulance? About that middle-aged woman's dead boyfriend? About the dad who nodded off forever? Is someone going to be relieved the boy's dad is dead too? She sits down. Her thoughts are all churning together, like magna. She worked eighty-three hours last week. And the week before, too.

She can see the steam rising from the mop bucket. It's December, after all. It's still sleeting. Cold, wet air blows right into the store, without that thick pane of glass. Damn. She should put on her gloves and coat with the neon *don't-shoot-me-I'm-not-a-deer* stripes. She should take care of herself before she takes any more care of any more mess. She always forgets to do that.

A police car pulls into the parking spot right outside the door. He rolls down his window. Leans out. Tasha smiles. Holds still. Lowers her broom as if it could be perceived as a weapon. She knows how to appear nonthreatening. It's second nature, but still unnatural.

Got the call about what happened.

Yeah. Pretty intense.

Those boys are real sorry. I have to ask you, do you intend to press charges?

Me? Charges? No. Wasn't it an accident? But I'm not the owner of the business. There might be insurance, and Tasha trails off, unsure what to say next.

Figured that might be the case.

Figured what?

That you aren't the owner.

Tasha sighs and thinks of the money she's saving up for her great-great grandchildren. Paying all she can forward so they won't be held back. The officer fumbles with his wallet and says, *Anyway, here's my card. Have the owner call me and tell me what he wants to do.* Tasha plucks the card from his thick, red hand, and snaps, *She will. And can you get my phone back? I loaned it to one of the boys during the commotion.*

Sure, he nods as he rolls his window up and drives away. She doubts she'll ever see her phone again.

It's not freezing, but close to it. The mop water is already cold. She gets a fresh, hot bucket. Her mother taught her: *Hot water cleans deeper. Fresh water cleans better. You can't get anything clean with dirty water.* She watches the glass bits slink down the drain, like flakes of gold in a prospector's pan. More silt for a fresh layer of world.

Nobody asked her name. Not the boys. Not the paramedics. Not the police. Not the woman with the coffin box. But she hadn't asked any of theirs, either. And that's just the way it is. Names turn jobs and roles into individuals, and that complicates things. Names are metamorphic.

There are plywood boards across a lot of windows around here. Protective bandages for dying places. The plywood would be bad for business. Bad for tips. Bad for Tasha's long game. She hopes Astrid can get the window replaced quickly. She needs all the hours she can get, so the years to come won't be so tiring.

Eventually, that bag of glass will become a gorgeous geological formation. Tasha's eyes smile as she pictures it getting soaked with some sort of neon-green antifreeze or the slippery, heavy-metal-rich water that flows under-ground. Maybe it will even become a gorgeous jewel someday. A rare gem. An artifact of an event no one in the future could possibly imagine.

She thinks of the long game that those boys are playing: hopefully, they'll band together and recover. Thrive, even. Hopefully, they'll leave something for their grand-children beyond a thin layer of plastic-trash sediment, and her grandchildren and theirs will be so far above today's omnipresent waste that they'll all know each other's names and say them gratefully, respectfully.

She looks at the card the officer gave her. Freddie. That's his name. That's her dad's name, too. In another era, maybe they could have been best friends. Someday. She hopes that she's alive during the early days of this geologic era, and not its waning moments.

She smells it before she sees it. Black smoke coming from the kitchen. The fire alarm howls. The cookies have burned. They're carbon now. Space dust, star-exhaust. Just like every other moving part, dead, alive, or dangling somewhere in between, molecular pawns in the universe's long game.

Eight in the Morning:

Olivia

She refreshes the online tracking page for the hundredth time. It was due to be delivered first thing in the morning. *First! Thing!* she'd demanded. *Boom. Yes. Finally.* It's there. The drop-shipper has taken possession. It will soon be hers. Finally. She has her coat and shoes on already. She's been waiting for this. Olivia dashes from her office to her car faster than the laws of time and space should have allowed her to. *It's here!*

This is it. This will save the hotel, revive the town, keep everyone and then some employed. Fill rooms. Move souvenirs. Spread all the good words. Put this town back on the map; take it to the top of the search engines. The sweetest cherries grow from trees planted where outhouses used to be, right? She pounds the steering wheel, victoriously hissing, *Let's do this. Let's do this. I'm doing this.*

It's her secret. Has to be. Forever. She'd already set up the game cameras. Helped her neighbors set up theirs. It would seem so natural. So unexpected. So perfect. So real. She'd told them it was for bears, to catch them in action. *It's not fucking bears! It's fucking awesome!* she shouts as she accelerates her car through a yellow light.

She's owned the hotel for five years. Bought the hunting lodge in the middle of nowhere, in Gour Borough, Pennsylvania, when she'd decided to move home, when she'd had enough of the vice fund. She'd traded stocks in booze, brothels, guns, pharmaceuticals, and tobacco companies. When the economy tanks, vice funds make massive money because vices make even the hardest lives easier to live. As the vice fund manager, she built a fortune on failing virtues.

She's no stranger to ethically ambiguous methods of earning a living. But this will be nothing compared to the vice fund. Nothing! This is going to be fun. Not quite clean, but good. Very good. Monstrous fun. This will make people happy. Bring crowds. No harm. She cannot wait to see it. She cannot wait. She rolls a stop sign.

She couldn't think of a better way to spend her marketing budget. How many postcards or brochures had she sent to travel agents? Tons. And what did they say? Same old lines. *Get away from it all! Rustic lodge! Great hunting! Full bar! Free Wi-Fi!* And who cared? Nobody, apparently. But this? People would fly across the world for a chance to see *this*. There'll be a waiting list as long as the *Bible*.

She went to the best costume designer she could find. A local woman, ironically, who she discovered while mindlessly scrolling Twitter. And the moment she saw the woman's work, she knew: *This is what I need.* She had it made to measure, made to her specific desires. She did it so, so right. With yak hair and real animal hides, with real antlers. No detail overlooked. She imagined how it would look on camera. That green, gritty footage of night-vision game cameras, how real and perfect it will be.

Stopped at a red light, she scowls at the thought of her stupid brother, who can barely manage to keep four part-time housekeepers employed at once. She thinks they'll all quit soon just to piss him off. Olivia snorts. Serves him right, the asshole. Once her hotel stays above thirty percent occupancy for a few months, she can fire her idiot brother and hire someone actually qualified to keep an eighty-room hotel in decent shape.

She winces at how dumb and awkward she must have sounded, when she described what she'd wanted, *Um, like a Sasquatch? But with antlers? And one big blue eye? You know, like the Old Man of the Woods? Unique. Not a yeti, more brown. And the actor, the actor is only five foot two, and slim. I want it to look sad, hunched over, and hyper-realistic. Better than CGI can do. And no pictures online. Keep this out of your portfolio. This has to be something nobody has ever seen before. And I'll need you to sign a non-disclosure agreement.* She pulls into the parking lot. Looks like somebody shot out the front window of that bakery. Probably insurance fraud. Numbers roll in her mind like gears. That bakery can't possibly make any money.

She parks across three spaces. It doesn't matter. The lot's huge compared to the number of its clientele, like every business around Gour—for now, at least. The drop-shipper also serves coffee, to make money in the early mornings when the exurban commuters stream into Pittsburgh. She decides to take a minute, play it cool, keep this as normal as possible. She orders an Americano, tips well, and sits at the counter, pretending she isn't so excited that she might just throw up all over the dusty packing supply display.

Her hometown. She'd come back to it. Out of love? Or spite? A bit of both. Nobody knew how much money she had. Nobody could possibly guess. Her brother thought he was doing her a favor, working for her. He'd never held onto a job for more than a couple of months. She didn't even have a mortgage on the twenty-acre property. She hadn't showered in three days and her jeans were from several seasons back, her shoes, even more out of step. She loves being in financial disguise. If and when she ever tells anyone about her wealth, it will be a sign of her trust in them, not an assertion of dominance.

The coffee burns the roof of her mouth, but she manages to pretend it doesn't hurt. *Don't make a scene. Not yet. Okay. Okay. Calm down. Relax. Don't be weird. Or, at least, try to be less weird.* She knows that when she puts it on she will be the best kind of weird. She will be the most beautiful kind of freak. The freakishness will be a massive electromagnet for business.

Olivia the math nerd. The kid who chewed her own hair. The kid with the one eye that never focused on your face. The kid with all the scholarships. With the lisp. With the funny hitch in her step. With the job in finance, in New York. With the creepy smile: three front teeth instead of two. With the hunched back. With the vice fund. That kid. That poor, hideous, clever kid.

Her best-known economics paper was on formulating mathematical predictions of known conspicuous behaviors as pertaining to long-term economic forecasting. To summarize: people pay more for what's rare (fine gem-stones, beachfront property). They pay more to be first at something (early adopters lining up outside of stores to get new junk). They pay to fit in and stand out in equal dollar amounts (all the clothes ever stitched). And they will pay a shit-ton for anything they can brag about having or having done. She did not use the term "shit-ton" in her paper, but said instead, "non-trivial income percentages." She paid the costumer so much.

Freak shows. Peep shows. Bearded ladies and stuffed dodo birds. Endangered species and celebrities. All the rarest works of art and nature. The reason fat becomes a liability as food becomes plentiful, and an asset when food becomes scarce. People like to look at what's rare and strange and hard to be. The Loch Ness tourism board has an imaginary dinosaur as its logo. People always want to see the freaky stuff. Kinks are expensive. So that's what she let the costumer think this commission was: a prop for a kink.

Her hands are shaking. She sips the coffee. *This is going to be amazing. This is going to reanimate this entire town. No, not this: Me. I'm going to do it. Me. Me. You're welcome, you idiots. You're welcome.* The best gifts are the ones where both the giver and receiver enjoy the transaction. She can already hear the cash register clicking continuously in the gift shop.

It's time to get it. To sign for it, to take physical possession of it, to really do this. She goes to the counter, says she has a pick-up. The cashier goes to the backroom. Wheels it out on a dolly. It's in a coffin. Oh, God. No, just a box that looks like a coffin. A box for a suit. She was expecting a bag. She's never thought of a garment bag as a body bag before, and now she'll never see one in any other way. She blinks and puts her hands on the pine box. *Okay, buddy, let's do this*, she thinks to the thing inside. She signs her name on the pick-up slip with a scribble and intense pressure.

The kid behind the counter helps her lug it to her car. It doesn't fit in the trunk, so she'll drive home slowly, with her hazard lights on, her treasure strapped to the roof with packing twine. *Should I tip you?* she asks her helper. *Naw*, he says. She gives him a dollar anyway. A dollar she earned by betting against human nature, by turning her vice fund into a monster that continuously vomits money.

As she slowly drives back to the hotel, she tells herself, *It's not every day you get to take home a fifty thousand dollar Halloween costume. Not every day you become the secret benefactor of your entire town. Not every day you get to walk around in the skin of something people actually want to look at.* She licks a tear that's rolled to the edge of her mouth.

She watches packs of kids tromping through the woods along the edge of the road in neon sweatshirts, in reflective coats. It's deer season. They're all hoping to kill something. It seems like it's deer season for most of the year. But not on her property. Not at the lodge. She'll be able to wander around, safe, in front of the cameras, like a freaky model on a muddy catwalk strewn with disintegrating leaves and fallen, rotting branches.

She cannot wait to see it. To touch it. To put it on. To become a part of it. She saw pictures of it, while it was in progress. She saw the sad face, the one, opaque blue eye bugling in its socket. The long hands with the bumpy knuckles. The black nails made of buffalo horn that flex over the fingertips and toes. The gray antlers that look like pieces of cold chalk. She saw how the fur was stitched and how the mask fastened. She loves it already. Loves it so much.

At her going away party, the night before she left New York, one of her coworkers had slurred at her, after a few too many fifteen-dollar cocktails, *Why you moving back to the place with the poison water? I mean, look what it did to you. Your face and stuff. Why go back there?* She'd shrugged at the time, but she knew. When a place is as much a part of you as you are of it, that's when you know it's your home. And that water? The thousands of traces of chemicals and heavy metals suspended in it? They made her both ugly and brilliant. Mutations aren't always monstrous. They can be startlingly beautiful, too, like the genius mind nestled in her misshapen skull.

She's driving so very slowly, so very carefully. Friends with newborns describe that first drive home from the hospital this way. Creeping slowing along the asphalt, stopping for longer than necessary at every intersection, fearful of all other moving vehicles. Well, this is probably as close as she'll get to that experience. This thing in the coffin? It's absolutely her baby. She clicks on her turn signal two blocks before she makes a right.

In her notebook, she'd copied down a bit of marketing advice, circled it, and jotted beside it, *this feels correct,* "First rule of hospitality. Make people feel comfortable. You put your young, smiley, pretty people behind the front desk. This isn't cruelty, or ugly shaming, or whatever: it's just a fact. Beauty is a comfort. It's a luxury good. It's a compelling feature of any service business." She's never worked behind the front desk. She set up her office in the back wing of the hotel where the laundry got done. She wants people to feel comfortable. She wants the hotel to work. She stays hidden.

The hotel was built in the 1920s as a respite destination for the robber barons and their silk-clad acquaintances to sip smuggled cocktails out of dainty crystal glasses. But now, it's in the middle of crumbling coal country, the land of wheezing Marlboro men who live in undriveable RVs parked behind shuttered malls. The lodge had languished under a receding economy and taken on the subtle aroma of wet mold and dry, mite-gnawed taxidermy. Olivia knows that it needs to be its own center of financial gravity. It has to be rare and attractive in a way that makes all of its sagging details part of its charm instead of its shame. Her car bounces over a pothole and she grits her teeth.

She wills her car up the rutted gravel road to the hotel. It looks merrily haunted in the December sleet: windows sparkling and white columns pert and brave against the gnarled trees that line the lawn. People will come in from Pittsburgh and beyond to stay here again. They'll open their wallets again. There will be signature cocktails again. It won't be so quiet in these woods for much longer. She pulls around to the back, parks near her hidden apartment, a hotel room without a view. The coffin is lighter than it looks, and she makes a mental note that the skin inside is hollow, empty, and not animated until she wears it.

Her brother's smoking near the dumpster. The more work there is to do, the more he dawdles in defiance of it. He's still the glowering creature he was in high school, the handsome, selfish family mascot. When he works behind the front desk, he flirts with and flatters the guests, absentmindedly manipulating them. His good looks give his pettiness room to flex and strut, mean he'll always get another chance. Olivia can't wait to fire him.

What the hell is that? he shouts in her direction.

Carpet samples. For the foyer, she lies. He lifts his cigarette and turns away, uninterested. He doesn't offer to help her haul the box inside. Another detail from her economic scholarship: people will work for less money if they think they're a part of something greater than themselves: e.g. nuns and fashion house interns. She won't have trouble keeping the lodge staffed once this effort takes off. The lodge will become legendary.

She pulls her curtains shut. Locks the door behind her. She should use a hammer to pry off the top, but she doesn't have one in her apartment. She jams a pair of scissors between the box and its lid. One by one the nails are loosened. She knows that experiences are more emotionally rewarding investments than equally-priced objects, and that linking objects to experiences results in products that can be sold at exceptionally higher prices. This is why people wrap presents: for the value-enhancing memories. She pauses to savor the unboxing, doesn't rush past the enjoyment.

She rejects superstition and bits of woo polished with essential oils and adorned by witch-blessed quartz crystals. And yet: as she opens the box, she feels something on a level logic can't reach. The mask has sad eyes and a humble mouth. Soft skin and wiry fur. Its hands are folded over each other, the way an actual body in a real coffin would be. It smells like lanolin and just-snuffed candles. She embraces it with the relief and understanding long lost twins feel in the moment they're reunited. *I've missed you so much. I'm so happy to meet you.*

She felt a similar pull when she learned the lodge was for sale. She didn't buy it because the financials made sense. She bought it because it made her feel enchanted. The lodge has a presence, a silent majesty. It has, and she hates that she thinks this, because it goes against all the mathematical knowledge she has, an alluring, vibrating spirit about it that says to her, *You are home. Welcome.* Something in her brain can sense things beyond the math of spreadsheets and the structures of grammar, and she assumes that has to be another gift of the tap water.

Her hometown is riddled with sinkholes and an opaque creek runs down its spine, but to her it's an enchanted forest, not a toxic piece of worthless real estate. And soon, she won't be the only one who thinks so. The fact that a statistically significant percentage of the local population exhibit physical defects by way of the heavy metals in the water supply will be left out of future marketing materials, but their presence will make its way into the legend of the place by word of mouth.

She peels off her jeans and sweater. She zips up the costume's belly. Fastens the mask to the chest. It's lighter than she expected, more like a cashmere sweater than a fur coat. She takes a few steps toward the bathroom. She gasps at her reflection, and steps closer to the mirror. It's so much more than a good fake. She is the real thing. She is the Old Man of the Woods.

She rests the artistically calloused paws on the edge of her mint green sink. Leans forward, bumps an antler into the mirror. No longer the hunched girl. No longer the girl with the bumpy skull and the low hairline. Not that kid with three front teeth. Now, she is unique not for her faults, but for her wild beauty. The creature in the mirror does not belong in the narrow, musty bathroom. She belongs in Penn's woods.

Before she put it on, she'd planned to burn it after it served its purpose. To destroy the evidence once the legend made the rounds and the films found their way to YouTube, once all the rooms were booked and the legacy permanently adhered to the lodge. But now that she's got it on? Now that it's even better than perfect? She would never harm it. Could never do such a blasphemous thing.

With her left antler, she pulls a curtain open just enough to peek outside. Her brother drops the butt of another cigarette. Waggles his ankle back and forth. She waits until she's sure he's gone back into the lodge, and then she waits even longer, listening to each breath she takes, feeling her palms dampen with excitement. When she's sure he's not coming back outside, she makes her way to the door. *I am going to book every damn room in this lodge.*

A constellation of seven motion-sensing game cameras is positioned across the property. If she follows the hiking trail, she'll be seen by each and every one of them. *Take one*, she thinks, *Roll film*. She has limited peripheral vision in the costume, and so she moves cautiously, stepping gently into the earth that's squishy from weeks of rain. She looks behind her. The footprints look like Hobbit feet. Perfect. Her deciduous forest is dishwater gray, and she blends in perfectly. The costume is not the same rusty brown as the local white-tailed deer. It's not the same slippery black as the rarely-seen local black bears. It's the same faded shade of gray as the bark of the maples and poplars. It's camouflaged perfectly.

She thinks about the t-shirt line she'll sell. About how she'll rent the rooms with the big windows for more money. How she'll sell plaster imprints of the tracks. How she'll have stuffed animals made with *Old Man of the Woods* embroidered on their bellies. How she'll offer DVDs of the collected footage, antlers on headbands, magnets, framed prints, bumper stickers, buttons, Christmas ornaments, tea towels. Oh yes, she'll need a gift shop. And an online store. And licensing contracts. Yes, she'll need all of that. She steps over a log that's fallen across a narrow hiking path. She's more graceful in the costume than she is without it. She smiles, but no one can see.

Metallic sleet drips from the trees, and as it seeps into her suit she begins to smell like a clean, wet dog: overtures of lanolin and tanned leather, a hint of something smoky. She swoons for the multi-layered musk. As she nears the first camera, she lowers her face toward the ground, rests her paw on the edge of a log. She imagines that the creature she embodies is searching for grubs, for snails, for forageable sustenance. *Ah, so, this is method acting*, she thinks.

When she worked on Wall Street she had nicknames. *Oracle. Troll. The Dividend Crone. Fetus Face. Gollum.* She knew all about them. The other women in the office had nicknames, too. *Quant-tease. Three Martini. Pay-to-Play. Zipless.* Olivia knew the power that came with being ugly. It meant she was free to do her job. She'd never be fired for not being too easy or too impossible to get. All she had to do was make everyone who ridiculed her piles and piles of money, and they would leave her mostly alone. She loved being mostly alone. She rests her right paw on a mossy tree branch, and moves like she is, finally, for once, beautiful. She enjoys it, because it's such a rare feeling, until she realizes how attractive beauty is, and she feels afraid.

A mutant deer crosses her path but is not alarmed. It does not scuttle way. It stops. It stares at her. His three antlers are far larger than hers, far more masculine, far more authoritative. As he exhales, his breath rises like her brother's smoke. Olivia squares her shoulders and shakes her head. He's elegant and powerful, but she's more unusual. Strangeness, she knows, is always a weapon made more powerful by its silent threat of possible madness. Lunatics. Drifters. Homeless people. Ugly women. People to be wary of because they don't have much to lose, and so they're free to lash out. The deer snorts. She raises her arms, not in surrender, but in acknowledgment: *Hey there, fellow rare bird.* The deer bolts away. She hears a game camera detect the motion and click, the sound of a cash register opening. She feels like a matador stabbing the bronze bull of Wall Street through its skull.

The deer had three antlers. Three. A taxidermist's challenge. A seventeen-point buck. Two where they ought to be, and one, in the middle, like a gnarled unicorn horn. The water still isn't clean. It might not ever be. She filters all the water in the hotel, gives bottled water to anyone who wants it. She drinks straight from the faucet. Her brother is ordinary, perhaps a bit of a jerk, but not an anomaly. But she, well she is an obvious mutant. Her DNA is kinked and knotted. She hopes no one ever shoots that deer. That poor deer: more a brother to her than her human brother could ever be.

A gunshot blurts out. Not on her property, but near it. It is deer season. Junior season, that short period of time where the young kids can take aim at the big bucks. Venison kept most families in the county fed all winter. Deer kill more motorists than drunk drivers. The wolves are long gone. The bears are in hiding. Internal combustion engines are the only real predator the deer face when they're not in season. Deer: the rats of the woods. Olivia realizes she'd never been against hunting, quite the opposite, a lot of hunters stayed at the lodge, but suddenly, she is keenly aware that she is not wearing anything fluorescent. From a few hundred yards, she looks like just another freezer-filling rat. She will not venture near the edges of her property.

Unlike the wide sidewalks of New York, on the narrow trails carved by deer, no one looks too long at her or looks away too quickly. She has all the space she could want. And this day, on this morning, at this moment, she aches for another deer to cross her path. She likes looking at something alive and having it look back at her, acknowledging her aliveness more than her otherness.

More gunfire. She hopes the buck with three horns will evade the armed teenagers. She hopes every freak would be fine. The boys with three fingers on each hand. The girls with the clubbed feet. The blind kids. The kids with the brain tumors. The kids who never learned to speak. The tall kids who sucked at basketball because their tendons didn't stretch. *Everyone, be safe*, she breathes into the soft skin that hides her lips.

A mechanical click. A camera sees her. Notices her. These next few steps mean the gift shop will never be silent. The money she earns in these next minutes will flow back into town, send all those odd kids to therapy, to college, to wherever they want to go. It will filter the water from those sickening wells, will solve everything, set it all right. All of it. She believes that her mutant self and her money will fix everything. It has to. Nobody else is stepping up into the woods. She walks toward the little camera that's nestled in a knot on an oak's trunk. As she does, she sees a flash of something: something fluorescent, something barely moving, something brilliantly, blindingly pink.

And that something, it sees her too. And it squares its little shoulders. It narrows its little eyes. It aims its little gun with its little, three-fingered hands. And it fires. Olivia crumples. The camera records. Her left antler snaps against a tree. She does not cry. She's too surprised.

The costume is stained. It is ruined. There is a hole in it, now: wait, two holes. Entry. Exit. One just above her right hipbone, in the front, and one in the back, again, just above her right hipbone. The bright pink thing rushes toward her, eager, hungry, proud, thrilled. Olivia bleeds.

Little boots are trampling brambles, coming closer. The pink fills Olivia's field of vision. A small child is kneeling before her. It's confused. *Oh, no, no. Oh, no. I didn't think you were real. Oh! Oh, man, oh man, oh man! Wait here. I'll be right back.* Olivia has no intention of waiting. The camera is rolling, and this footage is priceless. What hurts? A kidney? She has another one on the other side. An ovary? She wasn't using either of those anyway. Did it even go that deep? Was she merely grazed or mortally wounded? She acts as if it's not a serious matter. What hit her? A bullet from a kid's twenty-two? One level above a toy? Olivia groans. The little footsteps dash away. Olivia rises, propelled by adrenaline.

She survived all the taunting of all the grades of school. Weathered every insult. She jumped through every hoop ever tossed into her path. She is not abandoning everything for a child's day out pretending to hunt. She winces, hobbles back to the lodge. She turns to see the footsteps she leaves. There's no blood trail. It's all pooling inside the suit, dripping down her leg, soaking her right paw. She smirks. She's going to win this. Win big.

She can see the lodge at the edge of the trees. She hadn't gone far. Not far at all. The pain is motivation. She grits her teeth. Dammit, she loves her extra teeth. She loves her strange brain that elegantly crunches numbers. She loves this suit of supple armor. She loves her lodge, and the crumbly town it's tethered to. She winces with each step, denying that she's getting dizzy. *I will save you*, she says to everyone, including herself.

She thinks about civil war medicine, when legs and arms were amputated without anesthetic. She thinks of the pain millions of others have felt before this. *This is nothing. This is minor. This is mine.* She thinks of the gift shop. Of the YouTube hits. Of the new filtration systems she will build. She thinks of her brother, smoking near the dumpster, who has never thought of anything even half as grand as any of the things she thinks about all the time.

She wiggles her toes. Slimy. Blood's dripped all the way down. She trudges forward. Smirks. She's really hobbling now. Underneath her feet, under eons of soil, lie the bones of so many strong people just like her. Bones crushed by time and chemistry into sediment. Into soil. Just like the leaves. Just like the logs. Just like the ferns and bears and rabbits and sparrows. Just like the antlers of the deer who roamed these woods before her great-great-great-great-great and not-so-great ancestors touched foot on the continent. She owes them all to keep going.

She narrows her eyes. Sucks in the cold air. Leans on a tree. A few hundred yards. This is a crossable distance. All the ghosts of the woods are here, supporting her. She senses them, in the way logic cannot touch, cannot deny, or interfere with. She is animated by the sylvan magic she drinks straight from the faucet. She knows that that feeling, that strange animation, is why she owns this place. It's what she always wanted but never knew how to ask for. Her eyes no longer focus. She is no longer walking in a straight line. But she is making progress. The woods will not let her fall. The mascot never loses the game.

The driveway. She can see it. The door to her apartment. She sways. She wants some spirit to appear. The three-antlered deer. Herself as a perfectly formed human. But nothing crosses her path. This is the rare and special moment people pay for and wait a lifetime to experience. She knows this. Her thesis was right. Being this version of herself is the rare and wonderful experience she'd give anything for. She's going to sell so many goddamn t-shirts.

She's at the edge of the woods, leaning on an oak tree, breathing fast. She's almost there. Looking through glass eyes, she can see exactly where she needs to go. She's going to make it. She hopes that girl in the pink coat doesn't feel too bad. She wonders what the camera saw. She's glad her brother isn't outside. She loves this place. Loves the woods. Loves the thousands of souls that died and turned into the soil that snuggles so close to the sky.

The door. Her door. Unlocked. The suit has no pockets for keys. One broken antler. One hip bleeding. One elegant suit, stained and punctured after only one short wearing. All the cameras, up and running. One turn, and the latch opens. One step, and she is inside. Threshold: crossed. Her door: closed again. She moves one more pace, to the bed, a bed with a cheap polyester comforter just like all the other beds in the lodge, and she collapses on it, satisfied.

She knows not to sleep. Sleep, when wounded, is dangerous. No. She fights that urge. She fights for her lodge. For her town. For the kids who shouldn't, but still drink straight from the tap. She takes off the mask. Unzips the suit. Peels it from her body. Sees the wound. It's a shallow slice, maybe two inches long. Minor. To the shower.

She's dripping blood all over her apartment. But that's the great thing about owning a hotel: all the fresh, bleached towels you could ever want. She turns on the shower. She can't tell if the water is hot or cold. But it is her water: a light tea-brown, infused with everything she has ever needed and so many things she doesn't, and it will help her heal.

One washcloth absorbs the bleeding. She's surprised at how manageable the wound is, how quickly the bleeding is slowing down. Only raw skin and fat on both sides, no organs harmed. She got away with her prank; this investment will pay off. She drinks unfiltered water as it falls from the showerhead. She trusts that water, even if it destroys other people, because it has made her strong.

She knows first aid, and if there's such a thing as second aid, she thinks she can manage that, too. When she gets out of the shower, she will tape a dry washcloth to her body, and that will be enough. It's not bad at all. She's already feeling steadier. The scar will be a treasure. The bloody costume needs to be hung up, needs to get cleaned up and mended. She can't wait to collect the footage from the cameras. The girl who grazed her will be a compelling inter-view when the talk shows come calling. She looks up at the cracked plaster above the tub of her tiny apartment in the back of her barely visited hunting lodge and says to the entire tri-county area, *You're welcome,* as delicate tendrils of blood slip down the drain.

Nine in the Morning:

She's waded buoyantly through the woods all morning, the most gloriously miraculous morning in all of her remembered time on Earth. The ground, so wet and slick and thick with fungal life and dormant, deciduous potential feels so very right to the raw skin of her feet. She smiles so widely she drinks sleet. She is free and she is thrilled and she doesn't mind or even notice that she's been fumbling in circles for hours.

From the train, she'd thought she'd seen her house, but when she ran toward it, it obviously wasn't hers. The house she saw was crooked, mold-coated and dark, a cold-lipped-blue instead of the warm, royal blue she remembered. On she went, not recognizing how time had marred her mother's house. The air around her smells like home: the metallic haze of Gour Borough. She's been blissfully wandering in it all morning.

So many soft mosses and sharp ferns. So many tall poplars and short brambles. From understory to canopy, the woods feel like home. She is the Young Girl of the Woods, a creature once lost and confined but now freely on her way. Over the crest of a low hill, she sees smoke, a smudge of gray darker than the rest of the bosky horizon. Deer don't light fires in the rain. People do. People can help her get home. She aims herself toward the plume.

Her soaked pillowcase dress sticks to her lecherously. She looks more than naked. Her bare feet are numb. Her chapped hands tingle. Everything is thrillingly, tersely cold. She's free and the world is alive and she's sure that every kinked worm, mutant deer, and blind squirrel in the woods shares her delight in the gruel-blue morning light. Close enough to smell the smoke, she giggles.

She does not feel guilty for slamming a rock into the skull of her captor. She feels righteous, noble, like she is justice itself. She beams through sunken eyes, imagining how her quiet, nervous, fellow captor is on her way back to a warm, grand home. Amanda hobbles crookedly, carefully: the ankle that wore the metal cuff for so many years isn't quite stable. Her gait is floppy and uneven. She sees the tidy fire before she notices the one who started it.

Hunched near the trash-strewn fire pit where teenagers tell ghost stories and drink stolen beer is a moping teenager who she suspects can help her. He's loitering quietly, biding his time until his mother's boyfriend goes off to work and he can sneak back into his quiet, empty house. When kids in Gour Borough go camping, they want to get away from it all.

Sitting on a rock, poking his dying fire with a damp branch, he doesn't notice her. It doesn't matter if he's wise or simple, she doesn't need anything from him but his connection to the outside world. When he does hear her footsteps, light as they are, he stands up, throws an empty beer can into the brush, and staggers backward. Amanda doesn't realize how ghostly she looks, gaunt and obscene in the gray forest.

Thunder of a gunshot interrupts the meeting. Amanda freezes. Is her captor hunting her? Has her kidnapper risen from the railroad tracks? She crouches down and buries her face in spongy moss. She tries to be still, but she's shaking. The boy moves toward her slowly, arms out, as if he were trying to pet a feral dog.

The boy at the fire speaks gently to himself as much as to her, *Holy shit. Hey. You heard that: you know it's deer season? You need some neon. Here. What happened to you? Jesus. What happened to you?* He hands her a bright orange cap, warm from his own head. He wishes his mother's boyfriend hadn't locked him out of his house, that he hadn't wandered into that witch's shell of a house the night before, that he wasn't looking at this concentration camp looking kid right now.

If she, true justice, looked like a bald, stunted child in a wet pillowcase, then true kindness could just as feasibly be embodied by a greasy teenager having beer for breakfast in the woods. It was, after all, to her, a most magnificent morning. Anything could be real.

She pulls on the orange cap. Safety is a sensation kindness triggers. She feels supremely regal, coroneted by fluorescent acrylic. The boy looks at her and sees the old woman who invited him into her empty house. *People all kinda look like each other in Gour,* he thinks, *Not many families left.*

The wind shifts and campfire smoke perfumes her. She hasn't had a shower or a bath in more than a year. She's never felt so clean. Turtle Creek flows behind them, foamy and opaque, swollen over its banks. The world is full of so many delicious details that she cannot notice them individually. She is in love with everything, and she doesn't care if anything can be bothered to love her back. The boy's impression of her is filtered through his breakfast buzz, and he rubs his eyes, overwhelmed.

She'd never drunk filtered water. The truth of the filth in the ground didn't make the news until Amanda had been imprisoned at the sheep farm for well over a year.

The local elixir has changed her. Her mind marinated in it until her brain grew dense and strange and weird. Something made her unshakably optimistic and deliriously happy. That something: a viscous concoction of heavy metals and sloughed bedrock. Her mindset is unique in Gour Borough: she's physically unable to be unhappy. Even chained to a barn wall, she fell asleep wearing a grin. Her unclosing smile unnerves the boy.

He rummages in his backpack. His ancient, third-hand phone: damn, the battery's been dead for hours. But he is not entirely without assets. He offers her a flannel shirt because he is decent and she is not. It smells like campfire and open pores: a scent that she will forever associate with gentleness. The boy looks away as she peels off the pillowcase and pulls the shirt over her orange-capped head. She gasps with gratitude.

She's been gone from home so long. Do people believe in her anymore? Is she a myth too, like the Old Man of the Woods? Just because no one has seen her doesn't mean she's not there. She's always been there, just like everyone else has. He doesn't know what to do with this strange person, and he feels unsafe without his orange *don't-shoot-me-I'm-not-a-deer* cap. Invisibility is a liability.

Amanda's never thought of anything more magical or more perfect than the moment she's experiencing. The boy guesses that the sunken-eyed, pantsless girl who can't stop smiling is high on some chemical with a street value. He's seen the documentaries about child trafficking, about how pimps control their victims with drugs. He scowls on her behalf.

He doesn't know what else to do, needs something to do with his hands. He pulls another lukewarm beer from his backpack and cracks it open. He doesn't dare bring her back to his mom's house. Not with the boyfriend lurking around. That guy's eyes go dark when he sees girls. But he has to get her to somewhere. The woods are full of hunters.

He winces as he looks at her black feet, green bruises, gray scars. She realizes that she hasn't had anyone to talk to for eight years. The preacher? Never. Ruth? That just wasn't allowed. The sheep? They only pretend to listen. She moves her mouth, but it takes a while for words to form. She's out of practice at being a person.

But once she finds her voice, she speaks quickly, as if she'll never get another chance to, consonants hissing through the gap in her front teeth, *I'll bet my face was on milk cartons. I'll bet they sent out search parties with hunting dogs. I'll bet my mom offered a reward. Bet ya she did. I'll bet you everybody's still looking for me.* She doesn't state her name. She doesn't have to. He suddenly knows.

Her face is the face from the missing-person posters he helped the witchy woman burn. There's that reward for her: ten grand. He feels guilty for thinking of the bounty, but he could do a lot with five figures. He could get an apartment. Fix the differential on his mom's car and get her a washing machine that doesn't dance across the puddles on the basement's cracked floor.

I should alert the freakin' media, he mumbles. Amanda loves that idea. They can show up at a television station and run in front of the weatherman's map and tell the world hello during a live broadcast. Amanda's mother will watch and then run down to the station and they will reunite with a hug that lasts for days and the entire tri-state area will clap and throw confetti, blow up balloons, and believe in miracles. The boy gulps beer.

Amanda sighs as she rubs her purple ankle. She says with a giggle, *The crazy woman chained me to a wall. But I slammed a rock into her head, so we're even, I guess.* The boy thinks he should get her quickly to a hospital. Not the little clinic where they have condoms in a candy bowl. The big hospital, UPMC Presbyterian Shadyside, where the doctors are so good foreign princes fly all the way across the world for appointments. He needs to get her all the way to Pittsburgh, where there are people who will know what to do with her. It's less than an hour away, if traffic isn't terrible.

He can take his mom's car. He'll explain why later. Half a beer is almost enough to put out the campfire. The fastest route back to his house weaves through the woods where the deer hunters have set up shop. The safest path is along the railroad tracks behind the old hotel, then around the town dump instead of through it. She's worth four figures. He'll take the tracks.

I'll get you help, he says. He plans to carry her through the doors to the emergency room like she's a new bride and the hospital is their honeymoon suite. Respectable people will shake his hand and clap his shoulder and shake their heads at the awfulness he helped put an end to. The girl will get detoxed and cleaned up and sent home with clothes and antibiotics. He smiles back at her, proud of himself in advance as he motions to her, *Come on, let's go.*

Following him takes all her energy. He's taller and faster. She stumbles and hobbles, giggling as she tries to keep up. *This girl could collapse at any time,* he thinks. In his mind's eye, he sees her mother's haggard face lit from below by the flames of the burning missing person posters. The girl needs more than that woman can give. *The mom could probably use some time in a hospital, too.*

There's a sinkhole deep as a swimming pool in his mom's front yard and it gets a little wider, a little deeper, a little closer to the house every year. Her lot's considered an AML: abandoned mine land. Some long-ago shuttered company ravenously dug out the coal and left deep, hidden holes. He resents how obscene neglect is so easy to get away with. He hopes Amanda will recover, and that her mom has some insurance.

He pulls a half-full bag of generic Swedish fish from his bag. If he can keep her upright and moving, they'll both be better off. The candy in his hand confuses her. To her, it looks like a plastic toy, or some sort of bait. Eat it, he says quietly. After years of chewing sheep feed, the stale fish is a sticky, sensual revelation. Amanda begins to shake and cry. He's alarmed. She's euphoric. A game camera set up by the owner of the hunting lodge records both of them looking baffled in the fog.

The gist of everything he's been told in school is *Stay out of trouble. Don't be bad.* The ideal student isn't shown any ways to do that; just temporarily exiled in detention or permanently expelled if they step over invisible lines. The goal for kids in the borough is to be neutral at best. He inhales deeply, suspecting he might be able to become better than neutral if he can just get her to that high-tech emergency room in Pittsburgh. He pops a candy in his mouth and chews it slowly while he imagines the route he'll take.

His mom used to work as a cashier at the Shop-N-Save, but when its parent company was bought out all the rules changed. That place used to hire everybody. Even the kids with Down's could get full-time jobs bringing carts in from the parking lot. Now those jobs are part-time and require a bachelor's degree and a cover letter declaring a passion for loss prevention and resource management, whatever that means. Ten thousand dollars will go such a long way. He offers Amanda his hand.

Her stomach cannot handle the intensity of the candy's American-grade high-fructose corn syrup. The smile remains on her face as she heaves. Instinctively, he wipes her chin with the cuff of his sleeve. He's horrified, but tries not to show it, a skill he learned from watching his mother's boyfriend bleed out and dress deer carcasses. He picks her up and carries her down the railroad tracks like a toddler. *I got you. I got you.* Those words aren't frightening to her when he says them.

When his sister had her baby, he learned how to warm formula and change diapers. He was the one the baby liked best, even better than the soft, cooing ladies at the daycare behind the high school. He's patient and can soothe the insistent cries that make other people scream back. His sister moved out after a screaming match about mom's boyfriend. That baby has to be five or six by now. Amanda rests her head on his shoulder and closes her eyes.

She smells like farm animals. She smells ill. He doesn't mention it. He gets teased about how his clothes smell like the thrift store. But nothing smells more expensive than Band-Aids from a hospital. Nothing's cleaner, either. And if he has any say in the matter, she'll be covered in those soon. When he crashed his sled into a tree and broke his arm his mom had to sell the riding mower. He closes his mouth to shut out as much of the smell as he can.

I was with another girl, Ruth. She's quiet. Doesn't smile. She's littler. I like her a lot. He knew it. He knew there was some sort of sick trafficking going on. If you want to hide kids somewhere and do terrible things to them, what better place could there be than here, where even the kids who roam around in public barely get noticed? He steps over a *No Trespassing* sign and trudges up a hill.

He doesn't want to be another shirtless old man in overalls with a potbelly, haunting a porch. He doesn't want this girl to be another wraith on an exit ramp with a cardboard sign. He's going to write a college-entrance essay about this morning. About how he was challenged and he responded the right way. He knows the keywords for success from the all-school assemblies where the guidance counselor woodenly read from a standardized presentation she's required to give, but doesn't really believe is true, *Every good choice you make here is a step toward college credit.* He's going to get them both out of here.

How many nights had he spent in the woods this year? A dozen? At least. Curfews are for kids with parents waiting up for them. Half of his class sleeps on friends' couches or in damp tents on weeknights. He would have been on a friend's couch if everybody wasn't already out in the woods, aiming guns at forest rats. He's surprised by how light she is, how easy to carry.

Amanda wriggles free of him and hops to the ground. *This girl never stops grinning. What the Hell is she on?* Something's spooked her. He senses it too. The birds are quiet. It's so silent you'd think the sun stopped exploding, and that the silence stretched for light years. Then the forest rumbles: a sudden, unsettling ball of crunching noise. The hills are shaking and resettling: another little land-slide. Below them, an abandoned mining crevice gives way. She hops clear, but he falls into the fresh sinkhole. A trunk of rotted birch tree falls across the top of it, pinning him.

She's standing above him, still grinning. He's waist deep in sodden soil and rock, at least ten feet below her. Also collapsed: his unwritten essay about rescuing the damsel in distress. There's a devious pain in his left foot. The birds return to their chirping as he reaches up toward the tree trunk. Amanda shakes her head at how beautiful and horrible everything can look at once.

The tree trunk is slimy with moss, punky with rot, but he can get his arms around it. The soil is so heavy on his legs he can barely move. Amanda scrambles down into the pit and digs at his hip with her hands. *Look at all the worms in here! There are so many worms in here, so pink and happy!* she chirps. He feels nausea creep up his throat; chokes it back.

Woodpeckers and gypsy moths have had their way with the birch. It crumbles as he pulls on it. She's not moving much mud. He's already frustrated but Amanda is only beginning to work. Ruth took eight years to scratch through that single chain link. However long this task requires, Amanda's decided to accomplish it. He follows her lead and keeps trying.

He can wiggle his right foot; can shake off some of the earth. It's the left foot he has to worry about. His mom's boyfriend's closed-mouthed, narrow-eyed snickering comes to mind, uninvited. The boy strains and pulls and kicks the thought away. The ground smells like musk and kerosene, like the inside of a rarely-used machine shop. He's right above a pocket of dead air, foul with methane.

He feels that empty space below his right foot. He's in the top half of an hourglass-shaped hole; his foot dangling where time passes. More mud falls through the mouth of it, out of his way. He waves one arm at Amanda, *Get out of here. Get out. It's not safe. It's not solid.* He cannot, must not, let go of the tree trunk. Amanda does as she is told.

She climbs out exposed roots as footholds to reach the surface. The hole his foot is kicking opens wider. His pit deepens as soil falls through to the empty coal seam. The birch log is his best chance for getting out without further injury. It bows where his weight pulls it. His fingers sink into the rotten wood. Amanda becomes a silent, desperate spectator.

One good kick, and his right leg is free. He grimaces as he tries to move his left. Dirt is falling quickly past it, down into the bottom of the hole. He's hanging onto the birch, both feet dangling over the widening pit. Something has snapped inside his left boot. Maybe a tendon, maybe a small bone. He can't quite tell. He doesn't let go. That girl needs to be detoxed and his mom needs a new washing machine.

He struggles to climb up the trunk. Amanda is on her hands and knees at the top of the hole. She reaches for him and pulls on his sleeves as he inches up. He wishes she would stop smiling. Once he's past the edge of the hole, he rests his head on the wet ground, and his mom's boyfriend's snickering stops. He unclenches his fists and lets handfuls of rotten wood fall from them. *I knew this place wouldn't eat you. I just knew it*, says Amanda as she pats his shoulder.

He unties his boot to see what the problem is. No blood, just crazy swelling. He knows that if he takes the boot off he'll never get it back on. He laces it back up so the swelling doesn't get worse. Now they both need a hospital. He shakes his head. The reward money will have to go toward fixing his stupid foot. Amanda keeps patting his shoulder gently and says in her creepy-cheerful way, *I can help you walk.*

Even the most direct route to his mom's house is at least a mile long. But there's a road, not a well-paved one, but it's a road at least, at the bottom of the hill they're on. He recalculates. *Get to the road. Flag down somebody with a car.* He looks at Amanda's sickly, bug-eyed face, at her bloody ears, bare feet, and patchy clumps of hair sticking out from under his cap. They're both covered in mud. Hitchhiking is quite the long bet. But they have to try.

Together they hobble on one steady ankle each. When she smiles at him he realizes he's not altogether unhappy. He realizes he would be trying to get her to UPMC even if there wasn't a reward for doing it. Maybe he's already better than neutral. Maybe she's the only one who needs to know that.

The hunters are busy, sending bullets hissing through the woods. He hopes they don't hear any screaming deer. He's heard that rare sound before. It's the reason his rifle is rusting in the basement and he's not in a tree stand with his friends. It's another reason his mom's boyfriend snickers at him. The boy won't even eat venison.

I know it's winter because the forest is brown instead of green. The rain smells like snow. My birthday's in the summer, when the fireflies are out, Amanda gestures at the sky with her right hand, her left arm around his waist. His birthday's in the summer too, but earlier: when the aboveground pools start to breed mosquitoes. He remembers when Amanda first went missing. All the kids played inside that winter; the sledding hills were quiet; the locksmiths were busy. Then people forgot about the abduction, and the kids took over the woods again, but all the doors stayed locked.

They reach the train tracks. He touches one of the rails. If it's cold, no trains have rolled by in a while. If it's warm, one just went through. He looks both ways, twice. *Trains are faster than they look. I'm being careful. That's all,* he says when she's puzzled by his caution. His sister's baby's father died on tracks nearby, just before the baby was born. Nobody knows if he did it on purpose, but that's what everybody thinks.

Did you know that deer walk into the wind, so they can better smell predators?

Who told you that?

The lady who kidnapped me. Don't know if it's true.

It's true.

They sleep during the day too. I'd like to sleep today.

You will. Once we get somewhere.

We are somewhere already. We're here. I think it's nice.

I don't. I'm taking you someplace better.

They reach the edge of a gravel road. A row of half a dozen cramped Cape Cods are embedded in weeds across the street. He's pretty sure that most of them are abandoned, but he hasn't explored any of them on this side of town yet. *If you want to rest, we can stop here a while.* He needs to sit, to put his foot up and hope the throbbing eases. This feels like a fairly safe spot, no hills behind them that might crumble and crush them.

Amanda perches on a mossy rock. He leans against it, sighs. After the Swedish fish, he knows not to offer her anything to eat. He has no first aid kit, but he does have a couple of beers left in his backpack. He opens one and watches the road for signs of vehicular life. His foot feels slightly better, elevated.

If they go left, they'll reach the barely functioning gas station and then the dim little diner. If they turn right, the road will dead-end at the entrance to the train-yard.

He doesn't know if he can hop all the way, or if the girl can, either. He hasn't seen any cars drive by. He doubts any will.

You're not supposed to sleep if you have a concussion or are really drunk. She wants to sleep. He doesn't know exactly what happened to her or what chemicals are animating her, doesn't want to imagine any details. He nudges her, *No, no sleep yet. I don't think you should.* Awake is always safer than asleep. She isn't used to having a will of her own, so she sits up and stretches.

It's just light enough to see through the fog on the road. It's light enough to see that he needs to get her help as soon as possible. She's so thin he can see all the bones in her hands and the rings of her skull under her eyes. *Don't worry*, he whispers, *I'll get you out of Gour.* He wishes someone would make him the same promise.

Maybe they should start for the diner. The lady who runs that place is a decent type, like a mom from a sitcom or something. She'll know what to do, who to call. He'll split the reward with her. But that feels like such a long way. Maybe a car will come. He tries to move his foot in his ever-tightening boot, antsy to make the right decision. He looks at Amanda and then quickly away, because smiling back just doesn't feel appropriate.

He's never really done anything wrong before. But he's not sure if he's ever done anything terribly right, either. Survival isn't proof of goodness; it's just dumb luck. He knows that the longer he hangs around in Gour, sleeping on other people's couches and camping on school nights, he'll get less and less lucky and more likely to just lay down on cold tracks.

When my mom sees me, she's going to be so happy. She's going to cry happy tears. Big, wet ones. And she's going to hug me so hard. He hopes she gets what she imagines. Amanda stops talking. Her head jerks up, alert. He hears it too. Something near the house two doors to their north. It's upwind, but it's nothing predatory.

A metal screen door slams shut. A woman has just run out of the house. She jumps into a little blue Chevrolet. Amanda hears the engine turn over. The boy sees the taillights glow red. Then the woman jumps out, leaving the door open and the engine idling. She runs past the garage to the back of the house. The boy stands. Amanda follows his lead. He gulps, determined to seize this opportunity, to get her to the big hospital in Pittsburgh.

He wants to do the right things. To earn college credits with every choice he makes. He wants to help. But he also wants the entire reward. Besides: generic laws aren't written for people in unusual circumstances. He points his chin toward the little blue car. Camaraderie propels armies. Isolation drives mercenaries. Both forces compel them toward the car. Leaning on each other, they cross the street.

Ten in the Morning:

lice

She's late. Again. Late for that terrible job. The trash. She forgot to haul it out. She left her car running and has hurried to the back of the house to drag it to the curb. It can't sit there and stink for another two weeks. Thanks to the fog, she doesn't notice the two filthy kids who limp across the road.

She grabs the handle of the wheeled bin, full of two weeks' worth of nastiness because she forgot to do this last week, too. Who remembers to take the trash out when there's a funeral to plan? When there's an estate to settle? When you have to pick the least-stained dress to bury your mother in? She yanks it up the back steps. With every step, the lid pops open, and the stink of rotting food and soiled diapers wafts out.

She has to hurry. Her boss is a clock-watcher with all the charm of an ingrown hair, and those hotel rooms aren't going to clean themselves. Alice has had three hours of sleep in three nights. She keeps waking up, thinking her mother is still alive, still crying out for her. She waits awake in bed, listening for the not-there sounds of her mother's rasping. The final stages of dementia were the cruelest. Alice is trying to relearn how to sleep. She stumbles. The trashcan is unwieldy, just like everything else.

Alice never had enough money for a home nurse, so she went to work to pay for the rented hospital bed, for the diapers, for the sedating medication her mother needed to sleep deeply enough during the day for Alice to go to work. There are wilted flowers in the trash, cards expressing politely distant sympathy. She didn't want sympathy. She wanted help.

She comes around the side of the house and sees her car take off, tires squealing. Her phone. Her purse. Her keys. All of it. Zooming away down the street. The car turns and is gone. She sits on the wet curb beside the trashcan. She laughs. This fits, somehow, into everything else. She rests her forehead on her knees. She can't put together any words, not even inside her head.

No phone to summon the police. It's seven miles to work. No buses run out here. She had to be there five minutes ago. The low clouds look dark. Her house is locked. Her mother's safe, at least: not aching anymore. Doesn't need any more medication. Her mother's tucked in, nice and cozy, under a thick blanket of fresh sod, next to her dad, who'd been waiting twenty years for his wife to come and keep him company. Alice begins to walk: toward what, she doesn't know.

She was supposed to be in college. In a dorm somewhere, sipping coffee and highlighting a book, getting ready for graduation. But she'd promised. *I won't let them put you in a home.* She kept that promise to the woman who, in the end, couldn't even recognize her, who was afraid of her even as she spoon-fed her and wiped her clean. Alice didn't want to admit it, not even silently, not even to herself, but the fact was: she was relieved it was over.

A train rumbles through the woods behind the house. *It must have been some train hopper*, she thought, *a hobo or something.* Maybe one of the slow-moving junkies who wander around on the main road, near the shady gas station. Nobody else ever comes out here. Nobody comes down this street where only one house out of ten has anybody living in it, isn't boarded up. When the train depot closed a decade ago, everyone left. Except for her stubborn, deteriorating mother.

Even if she was an hour late, she could explain. Her car was stolen. Phone too. That's plenty of understandable trouble: more explanation than excuse. But she knows her reasons, whatever they are, won't matter. Her boss makes eye contact with her twelve inches below her nose and explains simple things to her like they're infinitely complex. He keeps her hours low enough that she'll never qualify for insurance. She steps around pothole puddles in the road, but her shoes get wet anyway.

Her mother owned the little, sad house outright. Alice made sure the property taxes got paid. She'd used her feeble college fund for that. She kept the lights and furnace on and she drove her mom to the doctors, who never had any good news. She bought the groceries, changed the diapers and she cried with the lights off. She paid the church and the stonemason and the cemetery. She washed hotel sheets and made hotel beds and cleaned hotel sinks and scrubbed hotel toilets and never complained to anyone but herself. She thinks she should become a lawyer, because that kind of work seems like the opposite of what she does. No cars have driven past her; nobody has come by to offer help. Do they ever?

She'd consigned most of the furniture. She sold the big, nice television, and kept the little old one in her mother's room. She'd sold her mother's big silver Chrysler and kept her little rusty blue Chevrolet. She'd even dropped the internet, which only reminded her that all of her friends were getting on with their own lives, anyway. She's stomping like an angry toddler, and it almost feels good.

In those last months, her mother had screamed at her in terror every time Alice said hello. *Who are you? Thief! Thief! Get out of my house!* Alice tried not to take offence, but she'd been raw-nerved and exhausted for months, and sometimes, she screamed back, *It's me, your only fucking hope!* which was not the answer her mother was looking for or an answer she was proud to give. She looks at the blank sky, hoping to think of anything else.

The garbage truck rumbles past. Alice runs toward it, arms flailing. *Please! Someone stole my car!* she shouts, *Can you take me to work, or, at least, out to the main road?* The gritty man behind the wheel shakes his head. *Sorry, ma'am. This ain't a taxi. Company policy,* as he drives off with the last of her mother's wet diapers into the back of his truck. Alice knows he isn't even a little bit sorry.

She'll never make it to work in less than two hours walking. And by then? Her job will be gone. She knows her boss has no more patience for her. She missed so many shifts with the funeral and the doctors. But tomorrow? No more crusty sheets. No more bloody towels. No more wiping and folding and aching. No more guests 'accidentally' walking out of the bathroom without a towel. Another layer of freedom? Yes. That's the best way to look at it. She'll try to sell the house. Go somewhere else. Far from Gour Borough. Away. Why not?

She can see the gas station around the next corner. The shady one, where everybody knows the junkies buy and barter for Oxycontin and the gas pumps are dry. Always open, not that she'd been in there for years. She'll ask for help there. She will solve this. Move on. Keep going. Her damp hair sticks to her face and the metallic fog is thick. She's going somewhere, and that's something.

That last month, her mother was barely a lukewarm skeleton. Her halo of white hair was patchy and wild. Her eyes opaque. Her hands curled like claws inside the terrycloth sleeves of her ratty bathrobe. She'd been Miss Murrysville, PA, once. Had long black hair and bright red lips and a laugh that could turn a thousand heads. Alice, when she can manage to sleep, has nightmares about both versions of the woman.

Alice's best has been shamefully inadequate. She was sorry she had to go to work. Sorry she didn't know who to call or what to ask for. Sorry about the bedsores and the way the bandage adhesive made them worse. Sorry about the big, gritty pills and how hard they were to swallow. Sorry she didn't make the beds correctly or fold the towels neatly for the guests. Sorry about the dirty dishes. About the smell. About the ill-fitting diapers and the yeast infections they caused. Sorry she was late for work so much. Sorry about how she sloppily wiped the showers out. About how the beds were made crookedly. About the brutal fact that she is just one person.

A pickup truck rolls through a pothole full of brownish-blue rainwater. The sludgy wave soaks her. She wipes salty grit from her face and wonders if she really is invisible. All signs point to yes. She'd begged for so much help. She made so many people uncomfortable with her requests for time, for effort, for anything. It was easier to praise her dedication than to lighten her workload. She knows that if she gives up now, everyone will say it's all her fault, but if she perseveres, she'll make the whole town proud. She wants to keep her future to herself, either way.

Rusty sleigh bells on the gas station door flatly jingle as she opens it. In Gour Borough, Christmas decorations stay up year-round. Disheveled on a good day, grotesquely exhausted on a typical one, and today: Alice is a damp, weary fright under the buzzing fluorescent lights. The shelves are mostly bare. Only a few packs of cigarettes and a few rolls of lottery tickets lurk in stock. A tall, thick man behind the counter is poking at his phone.

She blurts, *My car got stolen. My purse, my phone, my keys. I need the cops.* The clerk does not move with any empathetic urgency. He looks her up and down then casually dismisses her, *No cops coming here. Can't have that.* Alice's shoulders fall, but she understands. This grimy shop is just a front for pill sales. It's one of few profitable businesses left around. Maybe if she were Miss Gour Borough, or could pass for her, the guy would give a damn. He tilts his head toward the door, encouraging her to leave.

Alice does not turn to leave. Enough with being shooed away. Enough with being too inconvenient to assist. Enough. She wants something from him. She needs to be seen. She searches her coat pockets and comes up with a dollar in change. *Then sell me a scratch ticket. I have a buck here.* Her change clatters on the glass counter. He sighs as he scoops it up. If you want to participate in society, you've got to make monetary transactions.

He passes her a little cardboard square. When her mother was still alive, Alice would stop to buy scratch tickets at other, less sketchy gas stations, buying herself a few hopeful minutes away from home. She only ever won a dollar or two. But even when she lost, the moment of optimism before she scratched the silver film off felt worth the cost of the tickets. She never passed algebra two.

Her ragged thumbnail reveals one dollar sign, then another, and finally, magically: the third. It's not a jackpot, but it's something. She's won fifty dollars. She squeals as she hands back her ticket for redemption. *Well, shit,* he says, *Sign the back. Make sure you put your address on there, for the tax stuff.* He opens his register and counts out her winnings in crumpled, unlaundered bills. She signs her name quickly and illegibly and writes in the address of one of the boarded-up houses on her street. She has enough paperwork to do.

She stuffs the dry cash into wet coat pockets and leaves without saying thank you. Fifty bucks can cover the cost of getting fired, at least for the day. It's a tenth of the down payment on the kind of car that sometimes runs. It's a down payment on a flip phone. Yes. It's something. A sign of slightly better luck to come, she decides half-heartedly.

She walks past the Orthodox Church and its always-empty parking lot. Stuffy's bar next door is noisy and its parking lot is full, as usual. On Sundays, everyone prays for the Steelers at one of those two shops. Alice considers stopping into the bar and toasting her parents or her luck, but it's the first day of deer season, and she knows she won't fit in with the morning drinking camo-crowd.

Another block or so down the road, the post office. It's not open until ten. And further on, the diner. She hasn't eaten since, when, yesterday? The day before? And now she has money for anything on the menu. But first, she'll have to walk past the cemeteries across the street. Grandview, where the heathens rest, is beside St. Joseph's, where the believers are buried. Her family couldn't afford to tithe, so her parents went into Grandview.

That cemetery is tiny, less than an acre, and enclosed only by a picket fence that was white, once. There are no grand views here. Years of funereal trash slowly merge with the soil: faded plastic flowers, sharp wire wreaths. The plastic floral junk matches the faded Christmas decorations and political yard signs: all proof that someone cared about something once, but not anymore. She'll say hello. She'll tell them that her luck has changed. Optimism is her strongest and only defense mechanism. It only intermittently works.

Her parents worked until they couldn't anymore. Her father, one of the last men left at the Allegheny steel mill. Her mother, sorting mail at the post office until she forgot what her own address was. Alice was a late-in-life surprise for both of them. She never knew for sure if she was the good kind of surprise. They weren't the type to spoil her or each other with kind lies. Alice scans the field for the patch of fresh sod. *Hey, Mom.*

Her dad had the speedier exit: heart attack while mowing the lawn. Alice's mom found him sprawled in the yard, lawnmower crashed into the poplar at the opposite edge of the property, while Alice was at kindergarten. He'd only retired the week before. They had a sheet-cake at his retirement party and there were still pieces of it in the fridge at his wake. The fridge is empty now, except for half a bottle of ketchup and some pills her mom will never take.

She won't step into the graveyard. She hates the idea of standing on her mother's gnarled hands and her father's collapsed chest. She whispers across the acre, *Hey. Hi. I'm okay. I am. Yeah. I'm gonna get some breakfast, and then figure out my car situation. Yeah. It got stolen, just now, while I was getting the trash.* And she realizes nobody's listening, so she stops embarrassing herself on the side of the road.

Her mother's funeral wasn't well attended: just her and her mother's doctors, who are still waiting to be paid. Most of her parents' friends have moved away. Most of hers are off at college or have moved to where the jobs are. And the few people still around? They'd seen Alice struggling, noticed her mother withering, maybe even heard her screeching in the middle of so many nights? They were ashamed to not help, so they sent dollar-store sympathy cards to absolve themselves. The bouquets Alice picked up from the Shop-N-Save and laid at the funeral have blown away.

Alice wonders if, despite her best efforts, she's committed a crime. *Elder neglect? Is that a felony?* The rules are made for ideal situations, when right and wrong are clear and obvious. Just managing isn't an ideal situation. What are the rules then? If there's any evidence of a crime, it's all tucked into the sod, waiting for a tree root to tunnel through a pine box. *Caregivers need a lot of care too. Be good to yourself,* one of her mom's doctors had told her, without any guidance as to how. She wrings water out of her ponytail.

Alzheimer's takes a long time to complete its mission. If she starts West Allegheny Community College in the fall, she'll be a twenty-three-year-old freshman. If she graduates on time, she'll start at any law school that will take her at twenty-seven. Take the bar in her thirties. Pay off the loans for her education sometime in her fifties. By then, maybe she'd know for sure if she really is a criminal. By then, the statute of limitations will probably have passed. She hopes.

She doesn't know if the doctors and hospitals can try to collect from her, now that her mother's gone. She doesn't know if, because she had power of attorney, if she's responsible for all the fees. When she asked the nurses, they looked at her and shrugged. She wonders if she'll still qualify for student loans if she declares bankruptcy. She contemplates buying a big bottle of Nyquil with her winnings so she won't be able to worry about money for at least eight hours.

Her uniform is a black polo shirt and khakis she had to buy herself from the Goodwill. When she's on the clock at the hotel, she puts on a moss-green smock and becomes a woman named Housekeeping. She knows that one day, when she has her own business cards, with her own name on them, they'll be any color other than moss-green. And maybe someday, after she gets a different job, she'll buy herself a pair of jeans that haven't been previously worn. She's almost to the diner. She'll get out of the sleet.

As she trudges down the street, she thinks about all the guests who don't tip, about the doctors of geriatric medicine who didn't return her phone calls, about the local women in the Shop-N-Save who purposefully don't make eye contact with her. She would show them. What, she didn't know, but she would show them something. Eventually. Hopefully. Somehow.

The money feels like it's been in her pocket for a lifetime. Fifteen minutes ago feels like ancient history. And a week ago? A week ago, when she'd come home from work to discover her mother had died while she was folding towels? That seems like it had happened years ago, maybe even happened to someone else. She can't even remember exactly how she found her mother, and she knows that's her mind playing a defensive trick.

The post office is empty. No cars in the small lot in the front, three little mail trucks parked in the back. A gray box made of concrete. Metal bars cage the windows now, to keep the junkies from breaking in and pawing through the envelopes. She knows she has to leave and find someplace with more growth and less decay, where leaky above ground pools and cars left to rot on blocks are considered eyesores, not assets.

A few old pick-ups are stabled outside the diner. One of them has four mangy sheep peering out the back. *Who keeps sheep in a truck? Only weird rednecks in Gour,* Alice thinks to herself. The diner is warm inside, lit with yellow light. The coffee is on. The griddle is hot. The air smells like melting crayons. A few old men perch on round stools at the counter, complaining to each other about a world that doesn't want to hear about them anymore, passively watching the local news. Alice slides into a booth with cracked plastic seats near the front window.

Oh my god, honey! Did you get caught in the rain? Oh, Honey. Let me get you a towel. Oh, Honey. Coffee? Alice is startled. The waitress is twice her age, wider, softer, pinker, gentler. Alice nods and says, *Thank you, yes. Thank you.* The waitress brings out not only a little towel, but a big neon yellow sweatshirt, too. *Honey, now this is from lost and found. But you need it, you know, for deer season. Here. You'll feel tons better once you get yourself dry.*

Alice is overwhelmed. *Thank you. Thank you so much. You didn't have to, but thank you. So much. I mean. This is so nice of you. Thank you.* She wants to be that kind of person, somebody who gives gifts to waterlogged strangers. *No worries, Honey. This weather. Holy cats, will this rain ever stop? And here's your coffee. Warm you right up. Creamer's on the table.*

Alice heads to the bleach-scented bathroom, washes her hands and face with watery pink soap, and peels off her wet coat and black polo. The sweatshirt smells like fabric softener, like someone cares. In the mirror, she sees a face that isn't criminal, just exhausted. Her chapped hands rearrange her damp money in the sweatshirt's wide kangaroo pocket.

She orders pancakes, bacon, eggs, juice. She absorbs the warmth of the diner, and watches the clouds drift out of view. She doesn't want to think about the car or her mother or the bills. She just wants to sit and be normal for a few minutes. She'll go to the library next, read something for the afternoon. She'll ask to use the phone and call the police. She'll file a report, but she doesn't expect her car or wallet or phone to ever be found. The guys who run chop shops work fast.

Then what? She has no idea. She's never had enough free time to figure out what she enjoys doing, what kind of person she is and what kinds of things that person does. She looks at her reflection in the window and has no clue who's looking back. She can't help it, she laughs. The pathetically non-clairvoyant person she's looking at canceled her car insurance a year ago.

Alice feels the earth rumble. There have been a lot of little shakes lately, a bunch of rumbly mudslides. It's the old coalmines and underground creeks collapsing, the acidic soil around them saturated and fragile from all the rain. Her coffee cup rattles across the table. She wipes up the spill with a paper napkin. The old men at the counter whistle through their dentures. It's the most excitement they'll see for months. That was a big one.

On the other side of the Pittsburgh metro area, a traffic tunnel in the middle of the oldest and least maintained interstate in the country, Route 22, the Parkway, violently and completely disintegrates. Geology cleaves Pittsburgh's history into Before and After. A mountain suddenly, raucously becomes a pit, after a hundred years of underground decay, a hundred years of bedrock acidification. The entire Squirrel Hill Tunnel and the entire Squirrel Hill it snaked through collapses into a monstrous hole. The rain continues. Alice sips her coffee: weak but plenty hot.

Here ya go, Honey. I flipped an extra pancake for you. You look like you need a little something extra this morning. You remind me of me when I was younger. Loads younger. Hope that doesn't scare ya. Enjoy! Alice sputters more thank-yous. She hasn't had food she didn't make herself in almost two years. She smears golden butter across the top of the stack. The waitress was able to see her, and the waitress didn't look away. Alice will tip her so well.

Her mother's skin dissolves a bit more and her chest caves in a tiny bit further. Acidic rain rolls down nearby hills into Turtle Creek and turns it from bright orange to pinkish-brown. Alice knows billions of things are happening beyond her reach, and she sighs. She is just one, barely noticeable person. The entire world isn't her fault, and even if she tried, she couldn't save it. The bacon is magnificent.

On the other side of the glass, somewhere, the wheels on her car have stopped turning. Her phone can no longer vibrate with angry messages from her boss, who got his name changed to Housekeeping for the day due to her absence. The kids who stole her car aren't breathing under the weight of a mountain. Alice takes her time chewing the pancakes.

The waitress brings more coffee. Alice says thank you three more times. Her shoes are still wet, but her muddy pants are drying. She feels less dizzy, almost sleepy. She has no bosses, no dependents, nobody to answer to or clean up after. She has the rest of her life to do and be anything she wants. And because she has no idea how to even begin to research what that might be, she feels hollow.

The waitress leaves a blank bill on her table, and whispers, *This is on the house, Honey. Hope you have yourself a better rest of the day than the start of it.* Alice smiles as she chews. Her eyes water with gratitude. The waitress pats her shoulder and gives her a sad smile, *No problem, Honey. None at all.* Alice fishes five dollars from her wad of bills and leaves it on the table.

Orphan is a title you earn. It's not a word without a backstory, or a feeling that just anybody can understand. It's both a weight and freedom. Her mother lost her identity on the same schedule that Alice did: day-by-day, she became someone who didn't do anything but try to make it to the next. Alice eats a forkful of eggs and considers hitchhiking to the Greyhound station and begging until she can buy the cheapest ticket that will get her out of this time zone.

She sees a faded postcard taped to the front of the cash register, *Greetings from Destin, Florida!* She's never been to Florida. Maybe she can just walk there, take the Appalachian Trail or something. Migrate to a warmer climate on instinct, like a goose. The phone rings behind the counter. The waitress unplugs it from the wall instead of answering it. *Been ringing all damn morning. My cell too! I know I have bills to pay. I know. I just do not want to talk about it today.* The men at the counter snort in agreement.

She thinks about buying a decent bike. It'll be summer soon enough, and then she can pedal to anywhere. She'll be like those rich kids who take off for a year, to explore and brag about their leisure by uploading a thousand photos, only she wouldn't have a home to ride back to, or any fancy gear. She thinks about breaking into her own house, and finding nothing worth taking.

One of the old men at the counter shouts, *My Gawd!* and the waitress turns the volume up on the television. Helicopter footage. Frantic news people: national feeds, not local. Half a dozen ambulances with red lights flash on the screen. Cameras are reporting from the north end of what had been the Squirrel Hill Tunnel, only twenty or so miles away. Another one of the old men turns to Alice and points at the TV, *The tunnel collapsed! The whole damn mountain fell in! Holy shit! Another one adds, That's a toll tunnel. Poor gits paid good money to go get killed. Ain't that a kick in the ass?*

Scrolling across the bottom of the screen are the license plate numbers of the cars destroyed in the collapse, as recorded by the tolling cameras. The cameras know who drove to their dooms. A reporter tells the world, *I'm live at the former entrance to the Squirrel Hill Tunnel, reporting on the cave in. Reports are coming in that at least fifty vehicles have been identified as inside during the collapse. I'm told the landslide registered as an earthquake on seismic monitors, and could be felt for at least forty miles.* He's not standing in front of a hill. He's standing at the edge of a hole. Squirrel Hill is a valley now. A sinkhole big as a canyon.

Alice sees her plate number slide along the screen. The coffee goes cold in her mouth. She knows where her car is, where her phone is, where her purse is. Her identification. Her credit card. Would anybody ever realize that the crushed body in the driver's seat wasn't her? Would that person ever even be scraped out of that massive disaster? As far as the world is concerned, she's been crushed to death in a newsworthy tragedy and is now unable to pay any of those bills on her kitchen table. She feels absolved of everything.

That's what happens when yinz let yer infrastructure go to shit. My son and his buddies coulda reinforced that whole damn hill with local steel, one of the old men hunched over the counter grumbles. *Nah, this is bigger than yer boys could ever fix.* Alice sips some orange juice and has another bite of pancake. Her identity has been erased from the grid. She's as invisible as a living person can be. Her license plate number rolls along the screen again.

The reporter chokes back a mouthful of painful emotion and declares that the tunnel is completely collapsed, all four thousand plus feet of it. Traffic is being rerouted. Emergency management teams are now sending engineers and paramedics in helicopters. No one knows if the site is or ever will be stable. Alice watches ambulances turn their lights off and drive away from the scene, realizing there's no work for them to do. *They'll never get my car out of that. They'll never know.*

Alice waves goodbye to the waitress and the Greek chorus of old men and leaves the diner. She's been faceless, nameless, helpless, but she's never felt the freedom embedded in those details before. She pulls the hood of the garishly bright sweatshirt up over her head and disappears into her future.

Eleven in the Morning:

Caroline

Caroline bought the pencil case at the Goodwill that sells everything from worn out shoes to taxidermy supplies, as long as it smells used. She hadn't realized the case came packed with a pen and a jar of ink until she'd paid her three dollars for it. The long antique pen, carved of yellow bone and capped with a tarnished silver nib and the little glass jar of ink with its rusty green lid: they seem like haunted objects. But to Caroline, everything not brand new with tags seems spooky.

She asks a lot of slippery questions. *What criminal planted the crooked orchard by the railroad tracks? What secrets are buried at the bottom of the well behind the Orthodox church? Who is hiding just out of sight, behind every corner with black teeth and sick hobbies? Who stole my best friend?* She has good reasons to be nervous about what she cannot see.

During study hall, a dead hour created because the district just couldn't afford to hire any more teachers, she has nothing to do but fiddle and fidget and ask more unanswerable questions. She opens the case. The pen is smooth, polished, and it seems to fit perfectly between her fingers. She imagines that it's carved from the bone of a long dead witch who cursed the town before she was set on fire for public entertainment. Caroline dips the fragile instrument into its ink.

In the story she tells herself, it's a Ouija board without the board, this witch's pen. It's used for automatic writing, used to conjure words that cannot be spoken. The pen is warming in her hand, the ink reaching blood temperature. The nib is soaked. She takes a deep breath. The pen hovers over a sheet of notebook paper, and a drop of ink splashes and spreads tendrils across the page. Her headaches are coming more frequently and she is hesitant to tell her mother. She doesn't want to worry her.

It's been eight years. Eight years since Amanda's bedroom light went dark. She remembers how their fingers fit perfectly together when they held hands. The two girls with three fingers on each hand. Caroline's headaches started soon after Amanda disappeared. Her therapist assumes the events are connected. Caroline agrees. One missing child makes those who remain seem more precious. A close eye is kept on Caroline.

Caroline is sitting at the table alone, wearing the neutral expression she practices to avoid attracting attention. She needn't worry: the rest of the students are gathered around the television in the corner of the room, transfixed by the coverage of the tunnel collapse. She lifts the pen, closes her eyes, and feels her arm move toward the sheet of paper and lower the pen. She asks any ghost in the vicinity wordless questions.

She can hear the pen scratching across the paper. Her brain feels swollen in her skull. No one in the library notices her scribbling with her eyes shut. During study halls, the authorities lurk in the background, where they cannot mandate tasks or demand attention or ask annoying questions about spontaneous séances.

In a script not her own, she sees the words: UNDER TUNNEL. She does not know what that means. She closes her eyes again, and the pen aggressively scratches: LITTLE STOLEN CAR. She'd heard the news. The tunnel collapse this morning. She's just tired. Just exhausted. She can't keep staying up all night, avoiding nightmares.

She shivers. She sees Amanda, in a blink, in an image more vivid than a memory, but less real than a dream: the crooked smile from the missing person posters. Her friend who became famous in the worst possible way. Caroline had a chemistry test in the morning. She knows she passed it. She's not a strong student but she studies hard enough to pass for one. Survivor's guilt is profoundly motivating.

She shuts her eyes again. I WAS COMING HOME is written in larger letters, below the other text. She keeps her eyes shut, and the pen scratches a name: MANDY. Caroline looks away from the paper, sickened. She reminds herself what her counselor told her that everyone mourns in different ways, that mourning isn't something that's ever really finished, that it's normal to be overwhelmed when you least expect it.

Amanda's mother has withered into a watchful ghost, rarely leaving her home, just in case Amanda ever returns. The porch light didn't go out, even when the missing person posters came down. The search parties disbanded, and the detectives shelved the files. Parents stopped worrying about their kids getting snatched up by unnamed ghouls. But Caroline kept having nightmares about being buried alive, enclosed in dark silence that smells like wet stone, unable to see the yellow glow of the porch light.

Amanda's mother lives three streets away, in a little blue house that looks abandoned from the outside. Amanda's mother was soft and sweet once. Now she's all sharp angles and steely glares. When she sees Caroline, her eyes squint with jealousy and bitterness. Caroline is the opposite of Amanda. Caroline is still here.

Were you really in the tunnel this morning? Caroline whispers. She can't tell if she or a spirit is moving her wrist, if Amanda is there with her in the study hall. She closes her eyes, and trusts in whatever it is that's lurking in her space. She's not afraid. She wants to be helpful. She always wants to be helpful.

The pen writes: BLUE CHEVY. Caroline does not dare to peek at the text. Her knuckles are white. She is unable to unclench her hand. And the pen continues: SQUIRREL HILL. Her hand is shaking but the text is neat and perfect. Caroline inhales, shivers, and understands.

Caroline and Amanda used to race their bicycles up and down the street, eat popsicles on each other's porches. Braid their hair together and call themselves the no-piano twins, on account of their hands. They were inseparable until Amanda disappeared. There were no suspects that day or any day after. That year, bear hunting was reintroduced to the area, just in case.

This is all in my head. This isn't real. Her eyes still closed, the pen continues on, now scribbling with the thinnest line of ink, NOT IN YOUR HEAD UNDER A MOUNTAIN. The TV in the corner of the library spews the gruesome local news. Caroline hears more about the Squirrel Hill Tunnel as she stares at her page. She figured the words were her mind tying knots with random scraps of information. It can't be real. She squeezes her eyes shut as hard as she can.

The pen writes again: SAD WOMAN STOLE ME. Caroline's breathing is now shallow and fast. The pen scratches furiously: NO PIANO SISTERS. The pen falls from her hand. Her eyes fly open. She reads what her hand has written and feels her headache intensify.

She feels chilled, frightened, and dizzy. Caroline stares at the paper. She doesn't know what to do with it. She doesn't know if it's real or evidence of a crime or of sleep deprivation. The girls had joked, long ago, that maybe they *were* sisters. That maybe their real parents were another race of people who had three fingers on each hand, that they were some kind of changelings. They had joked, but the jokes weren't funny. The jokes matched their bodies too perfectly.

Caroline does not know any dangerous people, any creepy characters in town. She cannot name a single person she'd ever really feared. But once Amanda disappeared everyone seemed dangerous. Shadows seemed fleshy. Whispers became threats. She screamed when startled. She played inside. Read books on sunny days. Never unlocked her windows and doors.

Caroline realizes she is close to crying. She hadn't cried about Amanda in years. She thought that her wild grief had congealed into wistful nostalgia. She feels guilty, sometimes, for not thinking of Amanda every day. She feels guilty for using the loss of Amanda as a topic for an English essay. She feels guilty for being there, when Amanda isn't. She feels guilty for daring to write with the strange pen. She stares at the damp ink on the page.

The tunnel. A prime-time tragedy. A must-see disaster. She pulls out her phone, pulls up more news, just to check, just to see if what is written might be true. There's footage of reporters outside. Footage of a plume of dust shooting billowing out of the crater where a hill used to be. Footage of the drivers rolling into what they didn't realize was a tomb, just before the tunnel collapsed. The license plate numbers of the lost vehicles roll across a ghostly lane at the bottom of the screen.

Caroline squints at her small screen. She sees a little blue Chevy in the left lane enter the tunnel twelve seconds before the dust cloud emerges, twelve seconds before the toll road sign tumbles from the hill above the tunnel's mouth. *No,* she thinks. *There are thousands of cars just like that, rolling across the earth. Thousands. It's a coincidence. You're tired. You're so tired.*

She's afraid her hand might have written something wrong and true. She smells the wet rocks of her nightmares. She looks at her hands. A parting gift from a kidnapper who traffics in changelings? She wonders what she will say about this, if she ever says anything, to her mother. Her mother will worry and take her to another doctor. Her mother will treat her like she is precious because she remains.

She takes out another sheet of paper. She dips the pen into the ink. Her fingers curl around the bone. She whispers, *Mandy, tell me more. Tell me about what happened.* No one in the study hall notices. No one hears her talking to herself. She looks studious, intense. Nothing to see here. Another drop of ink falls, and she feels her hand jerk forward. This time, she watches the pen write.

WITH SHEEP ON HILL. RAN YESTERDAY. MISSED YOU. WAS COMING HOME. And beside the letters, a smiley-face. Caroline feels hot acid in the back of her throat. She doesn't know of any hill with any sheep. *Maybe I need to change my medication dosages again,* she thinks.

Caroline lets her hand relax just enough to control the pen. She replies, in her own, looping cursive: *I miss you, Mandy.* Caroline wants to do well enough for both of them, to be the pride of Gour Borough. She wants to build places with Amanda's name carved deep into keystones. She strives, strains, exhausts herself. Her extreme efforts have so far only led to deflatingly mediocre achievements. The medications can erode her anxiety but not her guilt.

Caroline's closure unravels. One answer, and now, a fresh cascade of questions. A little blue Chevy. It's now underneath thousands of tons of rock and soil. Will anyone ever dig it out? And what will be found if they do? How will they know it's Amanda? Will they? Whose car was it? The sad woman's? What kind of bone is this pen made from? Is it the finger she should have been able to point with?

I CAN'T COME BACK. If Amanda did come back? Her house, her town, her mother: all frailer and smaller, less civilized than when she left. Caroline feels embarrassed to picture her own life through outsider's eyes. *That's okay, you don't have to,* whispers Caroline.

The ink. It's a tarry concoction she sniffs and guesses is composed of fermented mink fur, lichen, and human hair. It smells like kerosene and vetiver and the metallic rot of Gour Borough tap water. Caroline imagines its origins to be spooky and cursed: that it was crafted by a wild woman a hundred years ago, a woman who never wrote down or told the recipe to anyone. Her brain can't stop telling stories in a voice that's never left her throat.

The voice shouts: *There's no more of this kind of ink anywhere in the world. Use it wisely! Listen closely! I have more to tell you.* She looks at the little jar and sees that she's used half of the ink already. She quickly screws the lid back on. She cannot name the voice. It's no one's she knows.

The pen wobbles like a chin about to cry, then rights itself. IT IS OK. The last letters are faint. The nib is drying. She disagrees with those six letters. She disagrees completely. A vine of panic is climbing up her spine. Her headache intensifies.

She can't let go of the pen. Just can't bring herself to release it. Can't move at all. *Mandy, don't you leave me again. I need you. So much. Don't you leave me again.* The pen doesn't move, doesn't touch the paper.

She listens to the reporters reporting live from the dead scene. Forty-eight vehicles were crushed in the collapse. The surrounding neighborhoods are being evacuated. There are calls for increased investments in infrastructure repairs and construction, talk of how the heavy rains of the last month had accelerated the dissolution of the hill's supporting limestone. Helicopters are circling the mountain. It now seems like a great landmark, a sacred place, a haunted grave full of more secrets than stones.

Caroline's eyes are heavy. She's exhausted by everything. She climbs out of bed every morning at five: after avoiding her nightmares, before the dew even settles. Her bus ride to the magnet school is an hour and a half in easy traffic. She does not complain. She does not dare. After all, she's able to be where she is, to do what she does. Mandy's not.

She feels guilty that she's able to go to her challenging classes, to study long into so many nights, to watch the sunrises and sunsets through so many dirty bus windows. She is guilty about all those things. Her head aches. She understands the sorrow in the voices of the reporters, some of whom drove through that very tunnel earlier that morning. *It so easily could have been me.*

Forty-eight vehicles. At least forty-eight people, undoubtedly more. The carpool lane was busy. Grief radiates through the greater metro area. And beyond the tunnel? How many loved ones die every day? How many unloved ones? How many unknown friends of friends? So many. Caroline watches the license plate procession and wonders which one Mandy rode in.

Amanda's disappearance is old news. Her name has faded from a white-hot topic to a nugget of hard-to-recall trivia. Old news and fresh headlines are becoming a chimera of a story inside Caroline's throbbing head. She's trying to make sense, to mash together pieces of two different puzzles. At least, she tells herself that.

The tunnel collapse is a tragedy vivid enough for spectators to attach their free-floating feelings to, like Amanda's disappearance allowed people who didn't even know her to cry. Caroline rubs her skull behind her ear, on the spot that radiates warm, tingling pressure.

She is writing so many papers, trying to memorize so many facts, practicing so many equations. She is checking as many boxes as she can. She's trying to be twice as smart, twice as good, twice as accomplished. She feels she has to be, for Amanda. But she's not twice as good in any way. She's a middling student at best. She thinks that's why her head aches so intensely so often, the stress, the guilt. She's wrong.

Her parents are relieved the teenager they've raised is too busy with books to get mixed up with bad crowds or illegal drugs or charming boys or unknown abductors. They admire her work ethic because they don't realize it's a masochistic penance. She studies so she can think about anything other than the one person she can't help but think about. But she hears Amanda's voice more than anyone else's.

She is always, automatically thinking about monstrous things that could have happened to her friend. Dark, filthy things. Horrid, vile things. Sticky things with wet, foul tongues. Oily things with groping fingers and leering, beady eyes. Things with grotesque and invasive designs on her body. She tries to hear the news over the babbling of her thoughts.

The coverage of the tunnel collapse continues. Even if it weren't blaring across the library, it would be continuing. Going on. Occurring. Everything keeps happening. Caroline will go to algebra class. Then she will wait for the bus. Then she will ride it all the way home as the sun sets. A stranger will try to talk to her. She will ignore him. At night, yellow light from Amanda's porch will creep across the street and cast angular shadows across the ceiling of her room, shadows she will stare at while insomnia harasses her.

What if the words written with the funky ink are true? Then tonight, while Caroline stares at her ceiling, Amanda will drip, crumble, and dissolve. The car she's in will, too. Forty-seven other vehicles will leak oil and antifreeze and blood into the deep, lightless ground. The mess will ooze into the water table, get digested by microorganisms and filtered by porous rock, and then rise back up through pipes and into faucets.

Caroline's grip weakens. Her knuckles shed their whiteness. She places the pen in its case. Stashes the ink bottle inside. Zips it shut. Takes two pieces of stained paper and shoves them into her history folder. She can't let her imagination derail her real life. She can't let the voices she hears make her crazy.

She arranges her hair behind her ears, wipes her damp eyelashes. She sees that there's a smear of ink on the edge of her hand. She quickly licks it, hoping to keep, to consume, to absorb some ghostly link to Amanda, some essence. It tastes like stale ash and black licorice. No one notices her do it. She feels like more of a weirdo than usual, and she whimpers, ashamed.

She knits her hands together, intertwining six fingers and two thumbs. Tonight she will take a sleeping pill and a swig of cloudy tap water to keep the nightmares from growing too vivid. Now she does what her counselor has told her to do when the anxiety creeps up her throat: she begins to count. *Ninety-nine. Ninety-eight. Ninety-seven.* The newscaster is announcing the names of the known dead. None of them sound familiar.

She no longer wants to shriek, but her heartbeat is pounding loudly between her ears. The spot behind her ear feels hot and angry. Eight years. Amanda spent eight years somewhere. Why was the woman sad? Was Amanda sad too? Will I be sad forever? *Fifty-three. Fifty-two. Fifty-one.*

Reporters impart background information: A two hundred-million-dollar renovation project was shelved last year due to declining tax revenue. The tunnel was known to have structural weaknesses. It was a tunnel built into a hill made of what engineers were horrified to discover: low-quality rock. A geriatric tunnel that had to be reinforced at birth with steel in order to be structurally feasible. It was now obvious that many abandoned mines intersected beneath the mountain, under the tunnel, full of acidic, corrosive wastewater. *Twenty-one. Twenty. Nineteen.*

Now they are commenting on how flat and blank the sky is, how many days it's been relentlessly raining, how perfectly sour the weather is today in Pittsburgh, and how quiet, how eerie the scene is, as sleet tamps down the dust at the mouth of the sinkhole. *Surreal*, they keep saying. *Surreal.* Caroline looks over her shoulder, more than half sure she'll see Amanda's gap-toothed smile beaming at her. No one's there.

Caroline has tried automatic writing before. She's tried everything to try to reach her friend from prayer to divining rods. But it's something unseeable, something no doctor or camera could ever detect, something strange and sacred and infused into her every cell that moves her hand when she writes with her eyes closed. It's never worked before, the automatic writing. She tries to close her eyes and see beyond herself, too. It's all working now.

Encouraged by what she feels, she silently vows to try this trick more often, to let her three-fingered hand transcribe ghostly sentences. She'll spend more time alone in her room, letting their words flow. The walls of her house will be marked with odd notations. Her parents will grow uneasy and afraid. Believing that what she writes is important, that any ink she uses is sacred, she'll beam like a holy oracle. Her mother will wonder if her daughter is unwell, if even the filtered water they drink is unclean. Caroline sees all this as clearly as she sees the television broadcast.

Because she has three fingers, Caroline's medical bills are paid for by the County Water Commission in accordance with a class-action settlement negotiated on the commission's behalf. Caroline can tell her mom that the headaches are worse, that she needs to see the doctors again. Caroline rubs her left temple with the back of her hand. A reporter begins to sob on live television.

She squeezes her eyes shut and sees what will happen as her skull is scanned. She'll go into the big hospital in Pittsburgh, where the doctors are so good foreign princes fly across the world for appointments. A doctor will find nothing unusual, and ask to subject her to an assault and battery of tests. Her mother will nod her authorization without blinking. Only a shaman could diagnose what afflicts Caroline, and none work at the medical center.

The doctor will tell her mother that he can prescribe medicine for the headache pain, that there's nothing more to he can do.

Caroline follows her story without opening her eyes. Her head will be shaved on one side. The more she keeps in touch with untouchable things, the less her head will ache. Her mother will be relieved and the doctors will smile and shrug, taking credit for the improvement. She will continue to be pen pals with ghosts, to doodle strange icons in the margins of her papers. It's impossible to excise magic with science. Not all of the water's gifts are insults.

She sees that by the following June, her by then unthrobbing mind will be hidden under soft curls and an itchy polyester graduation cap. She will proudly accept her cheap-paper diploma and smile evenly for the cameras. She will not be anywhere near the top of her class, and her otherworldly pen pals will tell her not to feel bad about that, not to feel anything but proud.

She looks beyond herself. Amanda's mother's house will burn down the day Caroline moves her tassel from one side of her proud head to the other. Caroline will go on to study geology and be mentored by a woman who wears a Fordite pendant around her neck and a leverageable chip on her shoulder. Caroline will learn how to reinforce bridges and she will scratch Amanda's name into steel beams.

She previews her graduation party. Caroline sees a strange creature: apelike, antlered, on two legs, and intuits that it is friendly. The town is small and will remain so even when it becomes famous for harboring such gentle monsters. Locals will sip signature cocktails at the famous hotel where it's rumored the creature lives. Caroline sees herself writing to Amanda about it.

Caroline inhales, and learns that her future smells like campfire. After the graduation ceremony, the graduates will gather in the woods around fire pits to drink lukewarm beer and toast each other's potential, to toast those who are no longer among their ranks. They will know that the place they call home is settled into their bones and they will smirk and promise each other that they will either leave and thrive in spite of it or belligerently stay and do all they can to make the musty woods flourish. None of them will admit to the magic of the place, but all of them feel it. She will high-four her friends who know she's odd and have never minded.

But before she goes to the hospital for tests she knows she'll pass, before she graduates, before she learns how to build solid structures on top of porous bedrock, Caroline needs to collect herself. She is no longer counting down to zero. She opens her eyes, and focuses on the future that's revealing itself to her in real time.

She's steady enough now to rise from her seat, and move closer to the television, where she hears more disbelief, more horrified amazement. She hears voices say that there was no way of knowing this could happen, no way to predict such an event. Caroline shakes her head. The reporters are incorrect. There are many ways of knowing what could happen: always are.

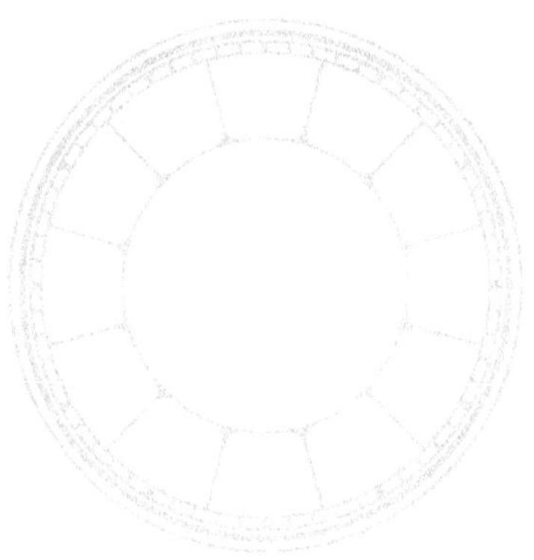